THE GUARDIAN

CELTIC CURSES

BOOK ONE

L.M. HATCHELL

The Guardian

Celtic Curses (Book 1)

First published by ALX Publishing 2023

Cover Design by Atra Luna Book Cover Designs

Editing by Two Birds Author Services
& Carol Tietsworth

Copyright © 2023 by L.M. Hatchell

For my baby boy and all the new adventures to come

CHAPTER ONE

"Remind me again why you thought bringing me to a graveyard would cheer me up."

Teagan gave me a sheepish smile as she pulled her trusty old Toyota Celica into a gravel lay-by that was barely wide enough to count as a parking space. The early morning sun shone through the windscreen, glinting off her shiny black hair, and her blue eyes sparkled mischievously as she cut the engine.

"It's peaceful?" she offered with feigned innocence. "Just a quick stop, I promise." With that, she climbed out of the car, her impatience to explore clearly getting the better of her.

I gave a martyred sigh but couldn't help the smile that tugged at my lips. Teagan and I had been friends a long time, and I'd known when I signed up for the girly road trip around Ireland that there would be at least a couple of random excursions thrown in for good measure. My best friend knew how to have a good time, but hiding underneath her carefree, fun-loving exterior was a history geek. Teagan enjoyed nothing more than exploring the weird and wonderful side of the past. Which apparently meant traipsing around creepy old graveyards.

Resigned to my fate, I squeezed out of the passenger side of the car and looked around. A number of other vehicles had pulled in along the narrow country road and I let out a low whistle. Old graveyards must be the place to be on a Saturday morning. Hopefully that didn't mean it was the local dogging site.

I hurried to catch up as Teagan disappeared between two large oak trees that marked the entrance to the church grounds.

As I stepped beneath the shadowy arch of branches, the graveyard sprawled out before me. Headstones were scattered around a field of overgrown grass. Some were little more than time-worn slabs of stone, others intricately carved Celtic crosses, or imposing statues of angels. All were beautiful in a somewhat morbid kind of way.

At the rear of the graveyard, the jagged ruins of an old church stood proud against the backdrop of a cloudless blue sky. Nature had welcomed what remained of the stone building with patches of moss covering its weathered surface, and the church blended into the landscape so well that it almost seemed to have sprung up from the earth.

"That's the Church of the Blessed Heart," Teagan said in a hushed voice as I reached her side. "For centuries there were rumours about witchcraft being performed here. Isn't it amazing?"

I shook my head in amusement at her barely contained excitement. "There's a word for people like you, you know that?"

"Taphophile?"

"No. Weirdo."

She laughed and swatted my arm. Then something to our right caught her attention and before I knew it, she'd disappeared into the distance, off to explore gods knew what.

I looked around. At least it was a pleasant morning. Considering the slow start we'd had to summer this year, a bit of fresh air wouldn't do me any harm. And it could be worse, I reminded myself; I could be stuck in the office buried in legal paperwork, or worse – back home, living with my mother, wondering where exactly my life had gone so wrong.

Finding myself homeless had been an unfortunate side effect when I ended my three-year relationship with Pete. He hadn't kicked me out of the house we were renting together, of course – he was far too nice a person for that. But after I crushed his heart to teeny tiny pieces by turning down his wedding proposal, I figured it was only fair for me to be the one to leave.

Guilt still choked me every time I thought about him getting down on one knee in front of me. I loved Pete. But I knew in that moment that I didn't love him the way he deserved. I couldn't resign him to a lifetime of less than he deserved, so I threw both of our lives into upheaval and prayed I wouldn't live to regret it.

Teagan had selflessly sacrificed her spare room so that I didn't have to face the torturous fate of moving back home and arranged this road trip to take my mind off everything. She was basically my guardian angel; the least I could do in return was humour her ghoulish detour.

The grass around the headstones was overgrown enough that it was easy to identify the regularly walked routes by the trampled patches that wound around the field. Still, I trod carefully, conscious of not stepping on any graves as I perused the worn epitaphs and unique personal touches that piqued my curiosity about the people buried beneath.

Unlike more modern graveyards, there were no neat rows here that made the place feel like a production line of death. The scattered, haphazard nature of these burial plots appealed to me, and though I'd never given my own future demise much thought, I decided I'd quite like to be buried in a place like this.

Would anyone notice if I slipped a placeholder headstone in?

Grinning to myself, I wound my way towards the ruins at the rear of the grounds. I was so lost in my thoughts that I didn't even notice anyone around me until I face-planted into a broad chest.

Hands reached out and grabbed my shoulders to steady me. Dazed, I looked up and found a man in his thirties with shaggy blond hair and the bluest eyes staring down at me. His tanned skin made him look like he'd be more at home surfing the waves than wandering around this old place, and it took me a moment too long to realise I was staring.

"Oh, sorry." Flustered, I pushed wayward strands of blonde hair back from my face. "I wasn't watching where I was going."

He released his grip, only for me to stumble as I attempted to step back out of his personal space. A smile tugged at the corner of his lips and his eyes seemed to dance with amusement as he steadied me again, this time waiting until I was firmly planted on two feet before releasing me.

"That's okay. You can bump into me any time."

I opened my mouth to respond – with something clever and witty, I'm sure – when Teagan called to me from the far side of the graveyard.

"Aisling, come here and look at this."

I turned to see my friend waving excitedly to me and cursed her poorly timed interruption. With an apologetic smile, I turned back to excuse myself, but the man was already gone.

Oh well, it wasn't like I was considering rebound options yet anyway. I ignored the twinge of disappointment and made my way to where Teagan waited beneath a cherry blossom tree.

"Look!" Teagan crouched down and pointed to a small headstone on the ground beside her. "Betty Anne. I was reading about her last night. She was accused of witchcraft and drowned to prove it. Of course, it was a bit inconvenient for the church when she actually died since it proved their theory wrong, but still they refused to let her be buried on sacred land. A group of local women petitioned the priest, Father Dominic, to step in and appeal their ruling, but he refused."

I crinkled my brow as I looked at the headstone. "So, how is her grave here?"

Teagan gave me a wicked smile. "Not long after Father Dominic refused the request, he went mad and tried to burn down the church, killing himself in the process. Rumours started circling that the group of women who had approached him were, in fact, a coven of witches and that they cursed him as punishment. When they were clearing up the damage caused by the fire, someone spotted this new headstone. No one knows how it got here, and nobody was brave enough to check if Betty Anne is actually buried beneath it, for fear of angering the witches."

I snorted. People believed the strangest things in the old days. Crouching down beside Teagan, I inspected the barely legible swirls of writing on the stone surface. I could make out the name Betty Anne, and there seemed to be an O'M after it, but the rest was too faded to make out.

"Do you know what her surname was?"

Teagan ran her fingertips over the letters. "There's been no reference to it in any of the articles I read. O'M. Could be O'Meara. Do you think she might be a relative?" She arched an eyebrow and gave me a teasing grin.

I laughed. "There have definitely been a few witches in my family, but I think that's more of a personality trait than an affinity for magic."

Pushing back to my feet, I looked around. Despite my misgivings, the place had a strange charm to it.

A flash of blue caught my attention, and I spotted the blond-haired man disappearing into the church ruins. Maybe there was something to this whole "interest in graveyards" thing if it attracted people like that.

"I'm going to explore," I told Teagan.

Closer to the ruins of the church, the graves became sparser – or at least less clearly marked. A low, crumbling stone wall ran behind the property, marking its boundary. On the far side, a wide open field lay. The green expanse looked remarkably bland compared to the church grounds where I was standing, but I found myself unable to tear my gaze away from it.

A shiver ran through me as something tugged at my chest. I *needed* a closer look.

I hadn't even noticed that my feet were moving in the direction of the boundary until I found myself swinging a leg over the moss-covered wall. The grass felt soft beneath my feet as I passed to the other side, and I was struck by the strangely uniform appearance of the field; all the blades of grass were the same height and the exact same shade of green.

A small voice at the back of my head warned that I

was likely trespassing on private property, but still something propelled me forward.

It was only as I grew closer to the centre of the field that I realised it wasn't all quite as samey as I'd initially thought. The ground ahead of me was raised, visible only now that I stood within a few feet of it. Odd that I hadn't noticed it sooner.

The aroma of fresh herbs drifted to me on the wind. Rosemary and a subtle hint of lemongrass. I inhaled deeply.

"Aisling. Aisling."

Teagan's call came from behind me, but it sounded muted somehow, as if I was underwater and she was calling to me from the surface. I turned to look back towards the church, but found my movements to be sluggish.

My friend waved to me from where she stood at the boundary wall, a frown clear on her face. I returned her wave with a vague gesture before my attention was once more drawn back to the raised section of the field before me.

Without really knowing why, I took the last few steps to the area of ground that was different from all the rest.

A shock of electricity jolted through me.

I gasped, and my muscles clenched in agony. All breath left my body, and one clear thought flashed through my mind: *I'm going to die.* Then everything went black.

CHAPTER TWO

Teagan gripped my elbow to steady me as she led me out of the hospital and into her waiting car. I wanted to tell her I was fine to walk by myself, but the protest had fallen on deaf ears the last three times I'd tried, so I knew it would be futile.

"We don't have to cut the road trip short," I told her when she climbed into the driver's seat and started the engine. "I'm fine, really."

"You collapsed and had a seizure. That most definitely is not fine!"

"The doctor said all my tests are clear. It was probably just low blood sugar. You know what I'm like if I don't eat."

Sure, I'd had breakfast before we'd left that morning, but stress can do strange things to the body, and I'd definitely had a stressful few weeks; maybe my sugar needs were just higher than normal?

Teagan pointedly ignored me as she turned the car around and headed back towards Dublin.

Exhaustion weighed down on me, and I slumped in the passenger seat, staring glumly at the sun as it set on the horizon. We'd been almost ten hours in a cubicle in the A&E department while doctors poked, prodded, and scanned me, only to suggest that I get some rest and maybe take up a hobby to help me relax.

That was a far cry from the fun road trip either of us had envisaged, and guilt mingled with the lingering sense of unease I'd felt ever since I'd awoken.

It had been unnerving to find myself cushioned by that strangely perfect green grass, Teagan's panicked face staring down at me. I couldn't remember how I'd ended up on the ground, and I had no idea how long I'd been out for.

The doctors seemed to agree with Teagan's assessment that I'd had a seizure; they just couldn't tell me why. Since I had no personal or family history of seizures, and all my tests showed up normal, they'd resorted to the standard diagnosis of stress. As much as the doctors' patronising tone had pissed me off, I had to admit it was preferable to accept that explanation over the possibility of something more sinister.

The vibration of the tyres on the road gradually lulled me into a boneless state of relaxation and my eyelids drooped closed. The surrounds of the car faded away and I suddenly found myself standing in the centre of that strange green field again. Hints of rosemary and lemongrass drifted to me on the wind, and though I looked around, I still couldn't pinpoint the source.

With the exception of the grass's eerie precision, the field was as bland and nondescript as I remembered it. Yet something felt different about it this time.

Energy crackled in the air around me and my chest tightened in panic as electricity tingled along the bare skin of my arms.

The wind picked up and, as it did, I heard a soft, rhythmic chant. The words were indecipherable, but they grew in strength and volume until, finally, one single word became clear: *protect*.

My chest constricted and I struggled to inhale. The ground beneath my feet shook and the scene around me blurred. A distant-sounding voice called to me, insistent, impatient.

I blinked in confusion, and the field disappeared. Instead, Teagan's face filled my vision, her brow creased in obvious concern.

"Aisling, wake up. We're home."

A knock on the bedroom door jolted me out of my groggy, half awake, half asleep state. The book I'd been reading tumbled from my face, where it had been resting, to the floor with a thud. I winced, hoping I'd remember what page I was on.

Teagan didn't wait for an invitation before she pushed the door open and looked in. Her eyebrow quirked up when she saw that I still hadn't moved from the bed. "Pizza's on its way and I'm opening a bottle of wine. If you're not out soon, I can't guarantee there will be any left."

As quick as she'd appeared, she was gone, her warning delivered.

I hadn't intended to follow the doctor's recommendation to rest quite so literally, but a long day spent in the hospital, followed by a restless night's sleep, had left me feeling less than enthusiastic about tackling the world today. I'd made a brief appearance to squirrel some food away and spent the best part of Sunday hiding away in a room that held little else other than a double bed, some built-in mirror-fronted wardrobes, and the remnants of my old life still packed away in suitcases under the bed.

With immense effort, I pushed myself up and swung my legs over the side of the bed. Maybe a shower would refresh me. It was only eight o'clock, and though I felt like sleeping for a week, every time I drifted off, I seemed to end up in that goddamned field again. It was enough to make me not want to close my eyes.

Ten minutes under the scalding spray of the shower and I was somewhat human. The buzz of the doorbell sounded just as I finished pulling on a fresh vest and shorts, and I opened the bathroom door to the irresistible aroma of freshly baked dough. My stomach rumbled.

Teagan stood in the kitchen with a slice of pizza

already clenched between her teeth when I emerged. She didn't bother looking up as she filled two large wine glasses to the top. There were none of those "proper measures" for us. We didn't kid ourselves; the bottle was going to be finished one way or the other.

Accepting the glass she held out to me, I grabbed a slice of pizza for myself, my mouth watering even before I tasted the heart-attack levels of cheese. I sighed in contentment, and Teagan grinned.

We took the pizza box and the open bottle of wine and settled down on the grey suede sofa that almost swallowed me whole it was so comfortable.

"I really am sorry about the road trip," I said when I'd finally satisfied my hunger enough to speak. Guilt had plagued me from the moment we'd left the hospital yesterday. Though I'd already apologised several times, I still felt responsible for her having to cut her holiday short.

Teagan waved away my apology as she had every other time. "The only thing I care about is that you're okay." She assessed me with an all-too-knowing intensity that made me squirm. "You would tell me if you weren't okay, wouldn't you?"

This time it was my turn to wave away her concern. "Nothing a good cheesy movie and some wine won't fix."

She clinked my glass with her own in cheers and picked up the remote control to switch on the television mounted on the wall. We settled in for a night of mindless entertainment, and I finally started to relax for the first time in over twenty-four hours.

The buzzing of my phone caused me to jump and I only just managed to stop my drink from spilling. I glanced at the screen and groaned as my boss's name flashed up beside the message notification. Why was he texting me on a Sunday night? This couldn't be good.

For a long minute, I debated ignoring the message. If I didn't open it, Clifford wouldn't get that stupid little tick that confirmed I'd seen his text. After all, I was meant to be on annual leave for the week.

But staff appraisals were coming up...

So, ignoring the disapproving look from Teagan, I gave a resigned sigh and opened the message. The words jumped off the screen, mocking me. I banged my head back against the sofa repeatedly and cursed myself for not choosing the "ignorance is bliss" option.

Teagan took a sip of her wine and waited for me to finish before asking, "What does Dickless want?"

I stifled another groan. "He wants me in the office tomorrow. A very important new client has requested a pitch at lunchtime, and he needs me to put together a presentation."

"You're on annual leave. And you're meant to be resting."

I scowled. We both knew Clifford didn't care about my legal entitlement to time off – ironic really, considering he was one of the founding partners of the law firm where I worked. If I refused to come in, he'd just get one of the other paralegals to put the pitch together and before I could blink, any chance of a promotion would be squished into the ground like a teeny tiny bug on the bottom of Clifford's shoe.

"Seriously, Aisling, why haven't you told him where to shove his job yet?"

"Smith & Mercer is one of the most prestigious law firms in the city."

My well-worn answer sounded hollow even to me at this stage, but I needed the stupid job for my newly single mortgage applications. So, I cradled the glass of wine in my hands and stared glumly at the telly as I mentally prepared myself to return to reality in the morning.

CHAPTER THREE

I stifled a yawn – my third in as many minutes – and took a sip of the black tar-like substance in the cup beside me. Coffee wasn't normally my poison of choice, but as the words on my computer screen blurred into an indecipherable mess, I forced myself to swallow the bitter liquid in the hope it would give me the energy kick I needed.

Teagan's disapproving glare had followed me all the way out the door that morning, and though I knew it would be career suicide, I'd seriously considered not coming into the office.

A couple of glasses of wine mixed with exhaustion had allowed me to finally get some sleep, but I felt less than rested. Any memory of my dreams had dissipated with the blaring of my seven a.m. alarm clock. The lingering sense of unease had been harder to shake, however, and the unbroken sleep had in no way rejuvenated me.

I scrunched my eyes closed and rubbed the bridge of my nose. It was only ten o'clock in the morning and already I was wishing the day to be over. With a sigh, I forced myself to focus once more on the brown folder that rested on the desk in front of me.

There was no name on the front of the file, only a small decorative F in the top right hand corner. My earlier perusal of the documents inside had confirmed that the company name was redacted throughout. That was unusual enough to have piqued my interest, but far be it from a lesser being like me to ask questions.

These companies were all the same anyway; they only cared about money. How much they could make, and how much you could save them when the inevitable court cases followed.

"Aisling, where's that presentation?"

My boss's barked question jolted me out of my musings, and I turned to see Clifford glaring down his nose at me from the door of his office.

Clifford Mercer had a remarkable talent for making you feel like something he'd scraped off his shoe. Unless you were one of the firm's high-paying clients, of course, in which case he dialled up the charm to sickening levels. Still, he wasn't as bad as the firm's other partner, and whenever I felt the need to tell him where to shove his job, I reminded myself of the promotion I'd been promised for the last two years.

Holding that thought firmly in my mind now, I pasted a smile on my face. "I'm just working on it."

With a huff to convey just how unimpressed he was,

he disappeared back into his frosted glass office. I gave his back my best death glare as the door closed behind him.

Right, back to making my boss look good. I returned to the presentation I had open on my computer and began typing. "Utmost discretion ..." Blah, blah, blah. "Client needs at the forefront of our priorities ..." Blahdy, blah, blah.

My body's muscle memory took over, and it wasn't long before the rhythmic click of the keys lulled me into a relaxed trance. At some point, the office around me began to blur and shift. The subtle hint of rosemary and lemongrass tickled my nose and a gentle breeze ruffled my hair.

I looked around, confused.

The office was gone. My computer, my desk, the chair that only moments ago had been so solid beneath me, all of it. Instead, I found myself standing in the centre of a stone circle made of large, upright boulders. Though the landscape was different than it had been in real life, I knew instantly that I was back in that same field beyond the graveyard.

A soft chanting penetrated my consciousness, and it sent a shiver of apprehension rippling through me. The sound grew louder until it was little more than an indecipherable buzz. I squeezed my eyes shut and covered my ears with my hands, trying to block it out.

This wasn't real; I wasn't really here.

I opened my eyes again – only to find a woman standing in front of me. She had long strawberry blonde hair and her eyes seemed sad as they met mine. There was something strangely familiar about her, but I couldn't put my finger on what it was.

Her lips moved as if she was trying to say something, but I couldn't hear anything over the chanting that now wrapped itself around us.

"I don't understand," I tried to say, my words swallowed up before they could even form a sound.

She reached out a hand towards me as if she might brush my cheek with her fingertips and mouthed a word that I thought might have been my name.

"Aisling!"

I jerked back at the barked sound of my name, and the image of the field instantly disappeared, taking the woman with it.

The firm base of my chair was the first thing I registered. The second was my boss glaring down at me from where he stood next to my desk. Anger made his already ruddy complexion turn puce and I swallowed, my mouth dry.

"My office. Now."

He strode away, no doubt in his mind that I'd follow.

I took a shaky breath, my fingers gripping the edge of my desk as I tried to reassure myself that it was real. Though the office seemed exactly as it should, I half expected to see the large standing stones that had only moments ago surrounded me, or the woman watching me with her sad smile.

What the hell had happened? Surely I hadn't dozed

off? Yes, I'd been tired, but I couldn't have just fallen asleep in the middle of doing my work ... could I?

Heart still pounding, I pushed back from my desk and prepared to face my boss's wrath. Legs slightly unsteady, I stood and turned for his office, the clock on the wall catching my eye as I did. I froze.

Eleven o'clock.

Nearly an hour had passed since Clifford last asked for the presentation. An hour that I remembered very little of.

My cheeks were still burning with embarrassment by the time five o'clock came. I sagged back into my chair and my eyes drifted closed for only a split second before panic snapped them open again.

Clifford had torn me a new one for sleeping on the job, and I didn't really blame him. I was still in shock that it had happened.

The walk of shame back to my desk had been almost as painful as the rollicking. Even now, the other paralegals cast surreptitious glances my way, no doubt imagining all the sordid reasons I might be so tired. How I wished my life really was that exciting!

It had officially been the longest day in history.

The god-awful coffee that I'd used to keep myself in a state of hyperawareness for the rest of the day buzzed through my veins, making my hands shake and my heart race. I longed for a warm shower and soft bed, but the thought of allowing my eyes filled me with dread.

With a weary sigh, I reached out to switch off my computer. Before I could hit the power button, Clifford strode into the office. I froze.

I'd gotten the presentation to him with five minutes to spare, and he'd been pitching to the mysterious new client all afternoon. Thankfully, that meant I hadn't had to face him again after my dressing down. But it also meant that my future at the firm had been hanging in the balance for hours. As I took in his distracted expression, I couldn't tell one way or the other how the meeting had gone.

With a longing look at the door, I waited for the inevitable barked order in my direction. Yet Clifford walked straight past me without even acknowledging my presence and closed the door to his office behind him.

Colette, one of the firm's other paralegals, raised her eyebrows in surprise at me, never once breaking stride with her typing.

Well, I sure as hell wasn't waiting around for Clifford to find another reason to yell at me, make me work late, or worse – fire me. I grabbed my bag, threw my jacket over my arm, and hurried out the door. If I was quick enough, I might even catch the early bus and get back to Teagan's at a reasonable time, with a job to return to tomorrow morning.

I joined the mindless swarm of suits trying to make a mass exodus from the city centre. As the week progressed, there was always a buzz about the city. Young professionals chatted excitedly about their plans for the future as they headed for one of the many popular pubs or restaurants to relax after a busy day. But Mondays were always slightly more subdued, with the weekend just a little too far out of reach.

A crowd had already gathered as I neared the bus stop and I rushed to join them, resigned to a cramped, sweaty journey home. I was so focused on my destination that when a hand landed on my shoulder and stopped me in my tracks, I let out a girly shriek.

"Sorry, I didn't mean to startle you."

I turned to find the blond-haired man that I'd seen at the Church of the Blessed Heart looking sheepish as he dropped his hand from my shoulder. His other hand held out a mobile phone that looked suspiciously like mine. You didn't see too many customised unicorn cases on phones these days... At least not ones belonging to adults.

"You dropped this." He held out the phone and recognition flashed in his eyes. He grinned. "You're the girl from the church."

My cheeks heated and I snatched the phone from his hand, suddenly embarrassed. He'd been at the church grounds. Had he seen me have the seizure?

"Um, yeah," I mumbled, trying for casual and failing miserably. "We have to stop bumping into each other like this."

His grin just widened as if he knew I'd happily

bump into that nicely toned chest of his anytime. "I'm Bres, by the way."

"Aisling," I offered.

The cheeky glint disappeared from Bres's eyes and he scanned my face, suddenly serious. "I was actually hoping I might bump into you again. I saw you collapse at the church and wanted to check you were okay."

So, he had seen it then. I cringed inside, but forced a grateful smile on my face. "I'm fine, thanks. Just all the excitement, I guess."

He laughed, but the intense expression never left his face. I was just about to excuse myself when he asked, "No side effects then? From the seizure, I mean."

My breath caught, and I was sure my smile had turned into a caricature-like expression. "Like I said, it was nothing. I'm fine. Now, if you'll excuse me, I have to catch my bus."

I turned from him without waiting for a response and hurried to join the crowd waiting at the bus stop.

C'mon, c'mon, c'mon, I silently urged the bus. I could feel those blue eyes watching me with curiosity, but when I gave in and risked a glance back to where he'd been standing, Bres was gone.

CHAPTER FOUR

"Are you going to finish that?"

Teagan barely waited for the answering shake of my head before she thrust the slice of garlic bread into her mouth. I laughed and sat back in my chair, too stuffed to eat any more of the delicious ravioli.

I'd been shocked when Clifford came to me this morning and told me to take a long lunch as congratulations for helping to secure the contract with our new mysterious client. Not one to look a gift horse in the mouth, I immediately sent Teagan a message and asked if she fancied joining me for lunch at our favourite Italian place, Il Vicoletto. Now that it was nearing time to head back to the office, though, I could think of nothing I wanted to do less.

The waitress came to clear our plates away and gave us a distracted smile. "Can I get you anything else?"

"I'll have a double espresso, please."

Teagan's eyebrows shot up, but she stayed quiet as the waitress hurried away.

I avoided her questioning gaze and instead busied myself folding my napkin back up. Though she'd stopped berating me for going back to work when I was supposed to be resting, I hadn't missed the concerned glances Teagan had been throwing in my direction more and more frequently over the past three days.

My sleep hadn't improved any, with that strange dream making a nightly appearance. Each time, it was slightly different. On Monday night, I could hear chanting and feel the harsh wind whip against my skin, but there were no images. Last night, there were images but no sound, almost as if I was watching through a sound proof bubble.

One thing remained the same every time – the feeling of unease that I woke with every morning. The heavy exhaustion grew worse by the day, and I'd even zoned out at work again this morning. If it kept happening, I wouldn't have to worry about my job for much longer.

"I heard you get up again last night," Teagan said, her casual tone not fooling me in the slightest.

"Oh, you know me. I have the bladder of an old lady. I just drank too much water before bed."

"You sure that's all it is?"

I forced a smile onto my face despite the dull ache forming between my eyes. "What else would it be?"

"You haven't been yourself since the seizure." She

held up her hands in a placating gesture, clearly noticing me bristle at the 'S' word. "I'm not saying there's anything to be worried about. I just think that maybe you should follow up with your doctor."

I sighed. I knew she was right. The truth was, I'd been trying not to think too much about it because I didn't like where that thought might lead. But at this stage, I was starting to feel like I'd lost my marbles, so a medical explanation nearly felt preferable.

The ache turned into a throbbing and I rubbed my temples. "I will," I promised, pushing back from the table. "I better get back to work. Clifford's generosity only extends so far, and I wouldn't want to push my luck."

We parted ways at the door with a hug, Teagan heading off for some retail therapy before her afternoon classes while I trudged my way towards the office.

Unusually for an Irish summer, the sun was splitting the sky, and I winced against the glare of it as I walked alongside the river Liffey. A steady stream of traffic ran along the road on the other side of me, but the noise of the cars seemed muted, far away. The pain in my head was still making itself known, and I idly considered the possibility that maybe it was because of all the coffee I'd been drinking.

A light breeze blew my hair across my face. I pushed it back and my steps faltered as the barest hint of rosemary and lemongrass tickled my nose.

No. No way. Not –

A sudden jolt from behind sent me stumbling off

the edge of the footpath and onto the road. My hearing returned to normal volume in time for me to hear the blaring of a car horn. I braced myself for the impact that was sure to follow, but a hand grasped my elbow and yanked me back onto the path. The sound of screeching brakes joined the horn.

A red hatchback skidded to a stop barely an inch from where I now stood. The man behind the wheel gestured wildly from me to the road and all around him as he roared obscenities. With more acceleration than was necessary, he tore off down the road.

Trembling and numb with shock, I looked from the receding car to the hand that still had a firm grip on my elbow. My gaze travelled up and my jaw dropped open.

"Aisling, are you okay?" Bres asked, his blue eyes shadowed with concern.

I pulled my arm out of his grasp and took a step back, nearly stumbling out onto the road once more. "Are you following me?"

He pouted, actually pouted, and shoved his hands into the pocket of his jeans. "A thank you wouldn't go astray, you know."

Anger replaced the adrenaline that was flooding my system. "Thank you for saving me from becoming roadkill. Now, answer the question. Are you following me?"

"No, I'm not following you." He ran a hand through his hair and had the grace to look sheepish. "I spotted you coming out of Il Vicoletto's and I was hoping we might talk."

"What is it you're so eager to talk to me about?"

He assessed me for a long moment, his gaze piercing. "I know about the dreams," he said finally.

My heart stuttered in my chest and it took all my effort to keep my features carefully polite. "I really do appreciate you helping me, but I'm afraid I need to get back to work. If you'll excuse me."

"They're not really dreams, you know that, don't you?"

His words caused me to freeze as I turned to leave.

"You've been trying to justify it to yourself – I must have fallen asleep, the stress is getting to me – but deep down, some part of you must know there's more to it than that."

My mouth went dry and I had to stop myself from wiping my sweaty palms on my trousers. "Who are you, and what do you want?"

"I want to help you." His eyes shone with sincerity and he kept his posture relaxed and non-threatening, but still his words sat uncomfortably with me.

"Let me guess, you've got the perfect cure for what ails me. All I have to do is sign over my life savings to you, and it'll be mine."

He gave me a crooked smile, and I silently cursed the gods for making it so that all the cute guys my age were either spoken for, crazy, or both.

"'Fraid not. I do, however, know why you've been having these visions, and I think it's time someone told you the truth."

I spent the entire afternoon at work restlessly watching the clock. Not willing to lose my job for being late, I'd cut the conversation with Bres short, but even though I knew he had to be a conman, that word "truth" called to me like a siren's song. So, I'd reluctantly agreed to meet him after work and returned to the office with so many questions filling my head that I thought it might explode.

"You have five minutes," I told him when he greeted me with a friendly smile.

Feeling stupid for even being here, I gestured towards one of the empty wooden benches on the boardwalk that ran the length of the river Liffey. Bres inclined his head and waited until I took a seat before doing the same. He said nothing, just stared at me appraisingly as if weighing a decision in his mind.

I shifted uncomfortably and looked around. I'd insisted on a public place for the meeting, and there were plenty of people nearby to help if he tried anything untoward, but I still felt oddly exposed as I sat there with his eyes on me.

"The clock is ticking. You might want to start talking."

He leaned back and rested his arm along the back of the bench. "What I'm about to tell you is going to be hard to believe. I'm just asking that you keep an open mind. Do you think you can do that?"

I said nothing.

"I knew there was something special about you when I bumped into you at the church," he said. "It was only when I saw you collapse that I understood what it was. I've been trying to track you down so that we might speak."

A shiver ran down my spine, and I wrapped my arms around myself. His flattering words didn't fool me; this was fucking weird. "How did you find me?"

"It's not too difficult to find people on social media these days."

"But you didn't know my name, so how –"

"The visions are getting worse, aren't they?"

My whole body tensed and my attempts to maintain a calm exterior no doubt failed. "I don't know what you're talking about."

"Yes, you do. When you crossed the boundary, it wasn't anything medical that caused your seizure – it was the spell triggering your dormant genetic memory. I can only assume, based on how blithely you entered the ritual site, that no one has ever explained the details of your heritage to you."

"Heritage? Spell? What the hell are you talking about?"

"You're the Guardian, Aisling."

I let out a harsh laugh, trying to ignore the cold sweat that had broken out along the back of my neck. "Guardian to what, exactly?"

"What's the point in putting a safety net in place if you're going to do a piss-poor job of passing the message down through the generations?" he muttered to himself rather than responding to my question.

He scrubbed a hand over his face and looked at me, his expression turning grave. "History has it all wrong. The Fomorians weren't really the bad guys. The Tuatha Dé Danann are touted as being this super race that came and liberated Ireland, but they weren't. They enslaved the people with pretty lies and controlled access to the land's magic so that no one would be in a position to oppose them."

My mouth fell open and I gaped at him, wondering if I'd blacked out again and missed some part of the conversation that would help his words make sense. Oblivious to, or despite my confusion, he continued.

"It took the Fomorians decades to amass the power needed to stand up to them. They were forced to sacrifice all magic in order to banish the Tuatha Dé Danann from this world, but they believed it was a sacrifice worth making for the greater good. Your ancestral line was tasked with guarding the barrier that holds them at bay." He gave me a wry smile. "Which you clearly knew nothing about since you're now looking at me like I'm crazy."

I made a conscious effort to close my mouth, but I didn't think I could hide the disbelief from showing on my face. Hell, I didn't think I cared. All this time I'd been worried about my mental faculties; this guy was a fucking lunatic.

Plastering a smile on my face, I stood. "I think that's five minutes up. It was –"

"They're trying to get to you through the visions. The Tuatha Dé Danann," he clarified. "The banishment spell tied your bloodline to theirs in order to create the Guardian. When you crossed through the illusion that shields the ritual site from the rest of us, it activated the link between you both. They're trying to use it to convince you to release them."

My eyebrows shot up. "Release them?"

Bres rose from the bench, clearly realising that I wasn't going to sit back down. "They want back into our world. They want to be set free so they can rule again. You're their way back."

An image of the woman from my dreams flashed through my mind, her eyes sad and beseeching. I shivered and pulled my jacket tighter around me, even though I knew the chill that had settled over me had nothing to do with the weather.

"I need to go." This time I did turn away from him, more than ready to leave him and his crazy story behind.

"They're not going to stop, Aisling. The visions will only get worse until they get what they want. Let me help you."

My steps faltered, but I squared my shoulders and kept walking.

CHAPTER FIVE

Leaning back on the pillows I'd propped up against the headboard of my bed, I opened my laptop. It took only moments for it to load up and a web browser to open. I stared at the flashing cursor as it taunted me, daring me to type. It was stupid. I knew it was. But try as I might, I hadn't been able to get the conversation with Bres out of my head.

Thankfully, Teagan had been at work when I'd arrived home yesterday evening, so I hadn't had to explain my preoccupation. That also meant, however, that I hadn't had anyone to distract me from my stupid thoughts.

I eventually gave up at nine o'clock and decided an early night was in order. Then the dreams came.

They were no more disturbing than they'd been on previous nights, but for some reason they seemed more real last night, more vivid. I woke before dawn with my bed soaked in sweat and the scent of rosemary and lemongrass still tickling my nose.

After trudging through yet another day at work where I walked a thin line with getting fired for incompetency, I'd come to the conclusion that I needed to put this shit to bed once and for all. So, despite my better judgement, I typed the words "Tuatha Dé Danann" into the search field and hit enter.

Results filled my screen. The headlines varied wildly, from references to the Irish mythological cycle to sensationalist comments about a super race of humans that were really aliens. None of the headlines made me question my sanity any less, so I picked one at random and clicked on the link.

Teagan loved everything history-related, particularly anything in the area of mythology or ancient civilisations. Me? I scraped by with a pass in history at Junior cert level and dropped it for my Leaving cert because I didn't want to write so many essays.

Still, I vaguely recognised some of the stories that were referenced; they were the fun myths we were taught as kids in primary school, before they decided it was time for us to grow up and learn about the more depressing side of history.

The Fomorians featured in many of the stories and, more often than not, they were depicted as monsters, the baddies of the story. Just like Bres had said.

Nothing I read suggested that either race had truly existed. I mean, come on, one guy was supposedly a giant with a freaky eye that wreaked destruction on whatever he looked at.

As I kept reading, a name jumped out at me from the text: Bres.

According to the website, which claimed to be the foremost resource on ancient Irish mythology, Bres had been the product of a coupling between the Tuatha Dé Danann and the Fomorians, an attempt to forge peace between the rival races.

I shook my head in disbelief. Did he think that by using that name I'd believe he was *the* Bres who lived millennia ago?

God, I was so stupid for even humouring this crap.

I had no idea how he knew about my dreams – because that was all they were. Maybe the dark circles under my eyes were a giveaway to someone talented in reading people. Because clearly he was a conman. And no doubt his good looks helped him lure plenty of unwitting women, but I wasn't that gullible or desperate for attention.

It didn't take a rocket scientist to guess why I was having weird dreams about the place where I collapsed. The seizure had been frightening, and though I'd been playing it down, I still had a niggling fear that there might be something more sinister behind it.

The solution to all this was simple. I'd make an appointment with my doctor, just like I promised Teagan. When the tests came back clear a second time, my imagination would have no reason to keep playing tricks on me. And once I started getting a proper night's sleep again, the weird daytime zone-outs would stop too.

I shut my laptop. It felt good to take control again.

Teagan taught a class on ancient civilisations on Thursday evenings and wouldn't be back for another hour or so. *Maybe I could make a nice dinner for us*, I mused as I left my room and headed for the kitchen. We could break out a bottle of wine and I could tell her all about the crazy conman that I now had stalking me, thanks to her strange obsession with old graveyards.

She'd tell me to go to the police. It probably wasn't a bad idea considering –

My phone rang and I jumped, letting out a curse as I pulled it from my pocket. I swore again when I saw my mother's name flashing up on the screen, then immediately felt guilty for my reaction.

"Hi, Mam," I answered.

"So, you are alive then?"

I cringed. It had been a while since I'd called her, and I knew the haughty tone was just an attempt to hide the fact she was hurt.

I loved my mam, but she'd become overbearing since I'd broken up with Pete. She wanted me to move back home, and only Teagan's swift intervention had saved me from that fate; we'd have been killing each other within days. Still, her concern was coming from a good place, and I knew she worried about me. That was the main reason I hadn't told her about the seizure.

"Sorry, things have been mental at work." Not really a lie. "How are you?"

I let out a relieved breath when she gave up on her interrogation and launched into an update on Aunt Betty's gout, the disastrous date she'd had after her friend had convinced her to try online dating, and the plans for the annual family dinner that was coming up in a few weeks time.

"And you're doing okay?" she asked when she finally stopped for breath. "I know you said you're fine after the breakup, but these things can take time to process. This will be the first dinner without Pete in three years. That might be strange. You could still ask him to come if you wanted."

I nearly choked. "I'm fine, honestly. And no, I won't be asking Pete to dinner. He suffered enough when we were together."

My mam chuckled.

In truth, we both loved the annual dinner. Any and all of the remaining O'Meara family had long ago made it a tradition to gather once a year to eat ourselves stupid and reminisce about stories from the good old days. Thinking of it now reminded me of what Bres had said about my lineage.

Feeling stupid and annoyed with myself, I asked, "Have you ever heard any strange stories about our ancestors?"

"What kind of stories?"

"Oh, I don't know, just stories that sounded really

far-fetched. You know how people used to believe in crazy things, like witches and whatnot."

"No, I can't say that I have. I do know that your great aunt Mary was fond of the odd tipple or two and swore blind to anyone that would listen that she saw ghosts. But that woman was off her rocker. Why do you ask?"

"No reason," I answered hurriedly. "Teagan was doing a project with one of her classes on family history, and it got me thinking."

I changed the subject back to safer topics and we talked for a while longer before saying our goodbyes. With a promise not to leave it so long to call, I hung up and stared into space, wondering exactly what kind of ghosts great aunt Mary might have seen.

CHAPTER SIX

The music was thumping and that second cocktail had gone straight to my head, leaving me feeling all relaxed and light-headed. When Teagan had invited me on a night out with friends of hers from work, my initial reaction was to decline. It had been a bloody long week, and I wanted nothing more than to curl up with a tub of ice cream and a crappy movie. But Teagan refused to take no for an answer; apparently my newly single status meant staying home alone on a Saturday night was illegal.

With the band in full swing, the crowd in Carroll's pub in good spirits, and the happy little buzz I was now on, I decided she'd been right – this was exactly what the doctor had ordered.

Down a random side street off Westmoreland Street, we'd stumbled upon the shabby little pub one drunken night many moons ago, and it had quickly become a favourite of ours. Though it wasn't far from the touristy hustle of Temple Bar, the drinks weren't expensive enough to require collateral on your house, and the live music was always guaranteed to draw in a good crowd.

Teagan was talking animatedly to a pretty brunette that she'd introduced as Sarah, and I waved to get their attention.

"I'm going to the bar," I yelled across the standing table that we'd managed to lay claim to. "Anyone need a drink?"

Teagan looked at her nearly empty gin glass, took a big gulp and gave me a wide smile that I took to mean "same again". I laughed and glanced in question at Sarah, who shook her head.

A wall of bodies stood between me and the bar, and the odour of sweat mingled with freshly poured beer as I carved a path through. I inhaled, the aroma oddly appealing to me, in a really gross kind of familiar way.

The queue at the bar was two deep, and I edged in behind a burly man with faded tattoos covering both arms. He turned, precariously holding three pint glasses between hands that showed a dusting of ginger hair on the back of them.

"Sorry, love," he said as he bumped into me, narrowly missing my shoes with the beer that sloshed over the edge of the glasses.

Waving away the apology, I sucked in a breath to make myself as small as possible as he squeezed past. That left one more man ahead of me at the bar.

I had all of a second to notice the nicely tapered

back and familiar dark hair before the man picked up his pint of Guinness and turned in my direction. My stomach lurched as I took in the black-rimmed glasses and kind brown eyes that stared out from behind them.

Pete, my ex-boyfriend, came to a sudden stop. Surprise flashed across his face before he regrouped and give me a tentative smile.

"Oh, hey. I didn't know you were –"

We both started, then stopped. I let an awkward giggle.

I hadn't seen Pete since I'd collected the last of my things from the house we'd rented together. Thoughtful as ever, he'd made the situation easy on me – something I probably didn't deserve. But there had always been such a comforting sense of familiarity between us that it felt wrong for things to be so strained now.

"You here with Teagan?" Pete asked, breaking the silence that had almost seemed louder than the din of the pub.

I nodded and gestured towards our table, where Teagan was once again absorbed in conversation and oblivious to my plight. "You could come say hi if you like." *Please say no.*

A pink blush crept up Pete's cheeks and it was his turn to look uncomfortable. "I, um, I better get back to Dean and Rachel. They'll be wondering where I am."

I glanced around and through the crowd I spotted the couple that had regularly been our double date partners sitting at a table on the far side of the pub.

They were talking animatedly with a blonde woman that I didn't recognise.

When I turned back to Pete, he was trying hard to keep his expression neutral, but I recognised the look of guilt in his brown eyes as he averted his gaze from mine. Something painful twisted in my stomach.

"I forgot, I really need to go to the toilet. Excuse me."

I didn't wait for a response; I hurried away from the bar and my ex-boyfriend.

Cursing myself, I made my way towards the back of the pub. I knew I didn't have any right to be angry or hurt, but dammit, it had only been a few weeks. Had he replaced me that quickly?

A bald, stocky man wearing a white shirt that looked far too crisp to be paired with his faded blue jeans stepped into my path just as I reached the door to the toilets. I looked up in surprise, about to apologise, but the words died on my lips when I took in his glower.

"We need to talk," he said, not making any move to let me pass.

I opened my mouth and closed it again, temporarily lost for words. I was pretty sure I'd never seen this man before, so why the hell would I need to talk to him?

"I think you have the wrong person. Excuse me." As I tried to sidestep him, he grabbed my arm in a bruising grip. I bit back a yelp.

"You *need* to come with me, Guardian," he hissed in my ear.

My heart rate shot up. Somehow, I found the strength to yank my arm away.

People around us were throwing concerned glances in our direction, so this time when I pointedly stepped around him and pushed open the door leading to the toilets, he let me go. The heavy black door swung shut behind me, instantly muting the sounds from the bar. I blew out a shaky breath.

The dark corridor was thankfully empty aside from the row of kegs that lined one side of it. There was a fire exit at the end, and I briefly considered slipping out and heading home. Instead, I made my way past the first wooden door on my right that had "Fear" written on it – the men's toilet (or for women who'd gotten fed up waiting in line) – and pushed open the second one marked "Mná".

How I'd managed to find the toilets completely empty, I had no idea, but I was grateful that at least one bloody thing had gone in my favour tonight. Moving to the white porcelain sink nearest me, I ran the cold water and splashed my face a few times, taking a moment to calm my racing heart.

Of course, I'd completely forgotten that my face was covered in make-up, and when I looked back up, I resembled something from a horror movie with mascara running down my cheeks. So much for it being waterproof.

I sighed and went into one of the stalls to get tissue

to dry my face. While I was busy rooting in my bag to see what make-up I'd brought that could possibly fix the mess I'd made of my face, the door to the toilets swung open. I kept my head down, pointedly focusing on my search.

Someone grabbed me from behind and yanked me back out of the stall.

Before I could scream, a large hand clamped down over my mouth, smothering any sound I might make. I struggled frantically, but an iron-clad grip wrapped around my waist and held both my arms pinned to my sides.

I couldn't breathe. *Oh fuck, what's happening?*

The ground disappeared beneath my feet, and it took my brain a moment to register the fact that I was being carried. Backwards.

Panic coursed through me and I swung my legs up, trying to get purchase on anything I could – the sink, the door frame, anything. My attempts were futile, and I found myself back in the noticeably empty corridor, being pushed towards the fire exit.

Sounds flooded in from the bar as the door to the toilets swung open behind me. I kicked and bucked; this was my chance to get help.

My foot connected with what I thought might have been a shin and there was a grunt of pain. The hand moved from my mouth, but before I could scream, the grip on my waist released and I stumbled forward.

Unable to catch myself, my head walloped into the edge of one of the kegs that lined the corridor. Agony burst through my skull and red exploded in front of my eyes. I gasped and reached out to steady myself against the wall.

Behind me, I could hear the sounds of a struggle, but the pain was so intense that I couldn't focus enough to turn and see what was going on. I needed to run, dammit.

A hand grabbed my elbow and a jolt of adrenaline shot through me, shredding all thoughts of the ache in my head. I turned, ready to claw the person's eyes out if I had to. And found myself face to face with Bres.

"Come on, we have to get out of here."

He tugged me towards the fire exit, and I yanked my arm out of his grip. No way in hell was I going anywhere with him. What was he even doing here?

The door from the bar swung open once more and I spun around, only then noticing an unfamiliar man dressed all in black slumped unconscious on the floor in the middle of the corridor. The bald man who had tried to intercept me only a few minutes earlier stood in the open doorway, a scowl on his face.

His gaze met mine for a moment before he noticed Bres at my side. Something like recognition flashed in his eyes before his expression turned steely. "You," he snarled.

"Please. You have to trust me." Bres held his hand out, allowing me to choose for myself.

I looked from the hand to the bald man who was now stalking towards us, and despite my better judgement, I took it.

We ran to the end of the corridor and Bres slammed down on the bar to open the fire exit. I didn't have time to register whether or not we set off an alarm before a blast of cool air hit me and I found myself running through the alley behind the pub.

My heart was pounding so loudly that I couldn't hear if someone was following us. I let Bres lead me out of the alley and back towards the main street and the comforting sounds of traffic before I finally skidded to a halt, panting.

"What the hell is going on?"

Barely out of breath, Bres came to a stop beside me. His eyes scanned the area for any sign of our pursuer as he ran a hand through his mussed-up blond hair.

"The Watchers of Danu. They know who you are now. You're not safe."

A chill ran through me and I wrapped my arms around myself. Did he mean from them or from him?

CHAPTER SEVEN

I gripped the steaming cup of hot chocolate in my hands in a vain attempt to stop them from shaking. At close to midnight, Starbucks was eerily quiet, but the glaringly bright lights at least gave the illusion of safety, if not the reality.

"Who are they?" I asked, finally looking at Bres, who sat across from me, sipping his tea and waiting patiently for me to compose myself.

"The Watchers of Danu are what's left of the Tuatha Dé Danann here in our world. They're zealots, a cult you could say."

I scrunched my eyes closed, trying to concentrate through the throbbing ache in my head. I'd agreed to come here with Bres after he convinced me it wouldn't be safe – for me or for anyone else – if I went back into the pub. That didn't mean I trusted him. And the idea that some crazed cult had tried to abduct me seemed like something from a bad movie.

It was only when we'd gotten to the coffee shop that I realised I'd dropped my bag during the struggle in the toilets. My phone, thankfully, was still in my jeans pocket, so I sent Teagan a message to let her know I was okay.

I felt terrible lying to my friend, but it seemed better to tell her I was upset after running into Pete than admit a truth I barely believed myself.

That same logic had stopped me from calling the police, despite it being the smart thing to do. I had no proof that someone had attacked me back at the pub, and everything had happened in such a blur that I wasn't even sure I'd be able to give a description of the man if I needed to.

I let a weary sigh. "You said the Tuatha Dé Danann had been banished from this world." Were those words seriously coming out of my mouth?

"The strongest of their bloodlines were. Some of their descendants were far enough removed from the main genetic line and the magic that they survived the banishment ritual. Their diluted genes make them no less obsessed with the cause, though."

"What cause is that?"

He raised an eyebrow at me, and I had the distinct feeling I was being chastised for not paying enough attention.

"They want to bring the Tuatha back to this world."

"And kidnapping me will help them do that how?"

"You're the Guardian. You may have been clueless

to your role in all this, but you're the key to bringing them back."

I snorted, hot chocolate almost coming out of my nose. "Are you really going to give me this 'you're the chosen one' bullshit?"

A smile tugged at the corner of his mouth and he slouched back in his chair, looking far too relaxed considering what we'd been through tonight. "Don't flatter yourself. There have been countless Guardians before you. You just happen to be the current one. If it helps your ego, I don't mind engaging in a little role play, though. You could find yourself a pointy stick to carry around and call yourself Buffy. I'll get myself a set of fangs and –"

I held up a hand to cut him off. "Please don't finish that thought."

Bres's blue eyes sparkled, but he obediently shut his mouth.

"Where do you fit into all this?"

"The role play?"

The stern look I gave him did little to dull the mischievous glint in his eyes. I crossed my arms and waited.

After a moment the cheeky grin disappeared and his expression turned serious. "It's complicated."

"Try me."

He was quiet for so long that I thought he wasn't going to speak. When he finally did, he wouldn't meet my gaze.

"My ancestors are tied to the Tuatha." He grimaced. "At some point in their history, the Tuatha and the Fomorians got bored with battling each other for control of the land. Neither race could get a solid foothold, so they decided to try a new approach. A truce of sorts. They arranged a marriage between a Fomorian male and a female from the Tuatha Dé Danann. That marriage was intended to produce an offspring that would unite the races. It wasn't a happy union, but the lineage survived."

I thought back to the stories I'd read online. When I'd read about the half Fomorian, half Tuatha Dé Danann offspring, I'd assumed Bres had used the name to try to trick me into believing it was him. But that was ludicrous, since even the most gullible person was unlikely to believe he was thousands of years old. If what he was saying was true, there was another, much simpler explanation.

"You're from that lineage."

He nodded, finally looking me in the eye again. "You're not the only one who's been screwed by their family history."

I digested his words. It still sounded absolutely crazy, and I couldn't believe I was even humouring the possibility that he was telling the truth, yet...

"What has all of this got to do with the stupid dreams I've been having?"

"Visions," he corrected.

I glowered, and he shrugged, looking wholly unrepentant.

"When you crossed the boundary at the site of banishment, it triggered a connection between you and the Tuatha. The connection was built into your lineage as part of the ritual, to act as an early warning signal of sorts, but it had lain dormant until now. They're trying to use that link to you to get free. The visions are their way of manipulating you into helping them. The only way to make it stop is by closing the gateway for good."

"Closing the gateway ... You mean lock the door and throw away the key?"

"That's as good an explanation as any. So long as the connection remains open, they can reach you. The only one that can close the access point permanently is you."

I frowned, feeling like I was Dorothy and had suddenly woken up in Oz surrounded by lots of small, funny looking people.

"Why create an access point at all? I mean, you make it sound like I'm the bouncer for some fancy club, that I can choose to open the door and let the Tuatha in, or tell them 'it's regulars only tonight.' It seems like a pretty big risk to take."

"The spell to banish the Tuatha took a lot of power – so much that it caused magic to disappear from our land almost entirely. There just wasn't enough to seal the gateway."

I cocked an eyebrow. "But there is now?"

Bres spun his mug of tea idly in his hands, something changing in his expression that I couldn't quite identify.

"The Guardian line was one fail-safe put in place by the Fomorians, but there was also a second ritual – one that would ensure the banishment was permanent. We've searched for a very long time to find enough objects containing a residual trace of magic so the ritual can be completed." He gave a wry smile. "Of course, we'd lost track of the Guardian line by then. I've been searching for you ever since."

The pain from bumping my head earlier in the night paled compared to the dull ache forming behind my eyes as I tried to comprehend the world he was describing. Magic. Super races. Rituals. It was insane, and any minute now someone was going to come along and tighten the straps on my straightjacket.

It didn't matter, though. All I needed was to stop the dreams – I refused to say visions no matter how much he insisted – and I could leave Bres to his delusions and get on with my life.

"And closing the gateway will stop my dreams?"

"It will sever the link between you and the Tuatha for good. They won't be able to contact you, or anyone else here in our world again."

I frowned as a thought occurred to me. "Why would you want that? I mean, you're part Tuatha, right?"

His expression darkened, and a shiver ran down my spine.

"I have my reasons."

A heavy silence fell between us. The adrenaline had left my body almost entirely now, taking with it the happy buzz from the alcohol and leaving only a harsh sobriety. I wanted to curl up in my bed and pretend none of this was happening, but that way lay dragons.

I was about to say that I needed time to think, when Bres met my gaze with those piercing blue eyes. "I can prove it if you'll let me."

CHAPTER EIGHT

Things normally appear different in the clear light of day. The monster that you imagined under your bed becomes a laughable joke once the first rays of daylight stream into the room. But the morning brought no relief for me. The unrelenting sense of unease weighed on me as I peeled open heavy lids, and a niggling fear insisted that the monster was still very much present.

I didn't even wait until I was fully awake before reaching for my phone and dialling the number Bres had me save the night before.

"Okay, I'll go with you," I said as soon as he answered, too on edge to bother with pleasantries.

There was a long pause before he finally asked, "Where do you want to meet?"

After agreeing on a meeting place in the city centre – there was no way in hell I was giving him Teagan's address – I got showered and dressed in record time. I guessed from Teagan's closed bedroom door that she was still sleeping off the night's festivities, and relief mixed with guilt as I slipped out without having to face her.

I opted to take the bus into town since I was too on edge to trust myself behind the wheel of a car. That came with the unfortunate side effect of having far too much time to think.

What was I actually hoping to achieve by doing this?

Bres had explained last night that he could prove everything to me; I just had to go back to the ritual site with him. Of course, the mere suggestion of that caused my sphincter to clench up in instinctual terror, but that was stupid. Wasn't it?

I could have collapsed anywhere. If I honestly believed it was the location itself that brought on my seizure, then I'd have to admit Bres was telling the truth. And that just added me to the list of nut jobs alongside him.

Yet, here I was, on my way to meet said nut job with butterflies doing somersaults in my stomach, and a single terrifying thought overshadowing all others: what if he really did prove it?

Bres was already waiting for me at the agreed meeting point when I arrived. He reached across from the driver's side to open the passenger door of the black BMW for me. His grin faded, immediately turning to a frown as he took in my appearance.

"Did you sleep at all?"

His blue eyes bore into me as I climbed into the car with a grimace. My dreams from last night were fading despite the vividness of them, but they'd left a pit of despair festering in the centre of my chest that was more terrifying than anything else I'd felt to date.

"A bit," was all I said.

He didn't push any further, and we lapsed into silence as the city skyline turned to motorway and then to narrow country roads. The closer we got to the old church, the more apprehensive I grew. I rubbed my hands on my trousers, trying to clear the clamminess from my palms.

"How can you be sure I won't have another seizure?"

Bres glanced sideways at me for a moment before returning his eyes to the road. "You crossed the boundary of a powerful illusion spell with no preparations. For anyone else, the spell would have acted as a deterrent. They'd have been driven away from the site without even knowing why. The connection you have to the site, however, acted like a magnet, drawing you to it. It was only your lack of understanding that left you vulnerable. That won't happen this time."

Still looking straight ahead, he reached over and squeezed my hand, a familiar cheeky grin tugging at the corner of his lips. "Besides, I'm used to ladies swooning over me. Don't worry, I know CPR."

I laughed and shook my head, some of my tension easing a little as I did.

We reached the Church of the Blessed Heart

sooner than I'd have liked – though any time would have been too soon. Considering how busy it had been last time I was there, I expected to see plenty of cars pulled into the narrow lay-bys on either side of the road. Strangely, the road was empty. Did the graveyard groupies take Sundays off?

"Come on." Bres flashed me a reassuring smile and climbed out of the car.

Feeling even edgier than I had been, I followed him, looking around at the eerie emptiness. The day had grown warmer while we'd been driving and the sun was shining in the cloudless blue sky above us; it felt wrong somehow for the day to be so summery and cheerful.

We made our way through the old graveyard to the low wall that acted as a boundary between the church and the field beyond. As I stopped and took in the view, I noticed yet again that the colour looked almost too perfect, too consistent. Was that part of the illusion?

"What now?" I hesitated at the wall, reluctant to take that last step over.

Bres reached into his pocket and pulled out a small black pouch. He untied the string that held it closed and an earthy aroma tickled my nose.

"Hold out your hand."

I eyed the bag with suspicion, but did as he said. He poured a small amount of soil into the palm of my hand, then retied the pouch and returned it to his pocket.

"This is soil from within the stone circle where the

ritual was conducted. So long as you keep contact with this, you'll be able to cross the barrier of the illusion spell without any ill effects."

"You're seriously expecting me to believe that this is magic dirt?" I asked, incredulous.

He chuckled. "Not magic, no. It will act as a connection between you and the land. That connection is stronger than the magic that remains here."

It sounded ridiculous, yet my fingers closed into a tight fist around the dirt.

"So, I just hold this and walk into the field?" My voice shook as I asked, and that now familiar mix of anger and frustration flooded me; a goddamned field shouldn't affect me this much.

"That's about it." He gave my shoulder a quick squeeze. "I'll be right here the whole time. I won't let anything happen to you."

I took a deep breath. His attempt at reassurance was appreciated, but I'd only known him five minutes and I had no idea what his word was worth. I'd either have to rely on my own nerve to get through the next few minutes or go home, forget about all of this, and stop acting like a crazy woman.

After a long moment, I stepped over the crumbling wall.

The perfect green grass crunched under my feet just as it had the last time. I forced myself to put one foot in front of the other, each step causing my chest to tighten further.

As I neared the raised area, a cold sweat broke out

on the back of my neck. I clenched my fist around the grainy soil.

I was so focused on trying to corral my panic that it took me a moment to notice the strange shimmer in the air. Had that been there the last time?

My momentum ground to a halt as a terrifying thought occurred to me: was I having another seizure? Was this how it happened last time? Maybe whatever was wrong with my brain was affecting my vision now, too.

The scent of rosemary and lemongrass drifted to me on a light breeze. I let out a pained groan. I didn't want to do this. Yet a strange tugging sensation in the centre of my chest urged me forward.

I closed my eyes and took a huge inhale, as if preparing to dive underwater. Then I stepped forward.

A sudden silence enveloped me.

I hadn't even noticed the cheery tweet of the birds, or the rustle of the wind through the trees, until it was all gone. In its place was simply nothing, almost as if I'd stepped into a soundproof bubble.

Part of me wanted to keep my eyes closed and remain oblivious. But that wasn't an option. So, slowly, I opened them and looked around.

Gone was the open field with perfect green grass. Instead, I was standing in a circle formed by enormous standing stones, just like in my dreams. The ground beneath my feet was blackened, and any remaining patches of grass were parched and brittle.

I turned slowly, taking it all in.

The church was still behind me, as it had been before I took that final step, and Bres still stood waiting at the boundary wall. There was an odd shimmery quality to the image, though, almost as if I was looking at it through water. Or through a curtain of illusion.

I sucked in a breath. Surely this wasn't real; I had to be hallucinating.

The aroma of rosemary and lemongrass was stronger here, but it had a smoky undertone to it now, almost as if someone was burning incense. There was no one in the circle with me, of course. And yet the memories of my dreams were so vivid that I could clearly imagine the circle that had been formed within the stone one. I could pick out the exact spot where each person had stood, the determined expressions on their faces not quite masking the fear.

I turned to the standing stone nearest me and placed a hand against the oddly smooth surface. The voices came instantly.

It was the same chanting I'd heard every night in my dreams – and more than once during my daytime zone outs. The words made as little sense to me now as they had every other time, but I could feel their power as energy prickled along my skin, causing the hairs on the back of my neck to raise.

I pulled back, gasping for air. It was all true.

CHAPTER NINE

The silence in the car held a new weight as we drove away from the Church of the Blessed Heart. Bres kept his focus on the road ahead, giving me time to process what I'd seen. I was sure he was only dying to say "I told you so" or ask if I finally believed, but then again, maybe he was satisfied that his proof spoke for itself.

And it did. What I'd seen in the field spoke volumes. I just couldn't decide exactly what it was saying to me.

There was such sadness to the place that it left me feeling hollow when I finally stepped back past the illusion. But whose sorrow? Mine? The Tuatha Dé Danann's? The Fomorians'? The land's?

It was still possible that this was all a delusion caused by some brain damage linked to my seizure. That would be the more sensible explanation – though no less terrifying. Yet, I couldn't deny what I'd seen with my very eyes. And I couldn't deny what I felt.

The soil that had allowed me to pass through the illusion rested in my jacket pocket like a grenade with the pin pulled. I'd wrapped it up in a clean tissue and put it there when Bres wasn't looking. I wasn't really sure why I was doing it, but for some reason, I was reluctant to let it go.

I leaned my head against the passenger window and let the cool glass ease some of the dull ache that was once more building in my head.

"How did you know about all of this?"

I hated that my voice sounded so defeated, but I was so bloody weary. I'd been convinced that he was a nut job, spinning some fanciful tale in an attempt to con me out of my not-so-vast fortune. Every logical part of my being insisted that there was a simple explanation for the situation, but that conviction was growing shakier by the minute.

"Your family didn't do a very good job of passing down your history. Mine went to the opposite extreme." He grimaced, his grip tightening on the steering wheel for a moment before he forced it to relax. "I've had these stories drilled into me since I was a child. Normal kids had the bogeyman to scare them in the dark of night. I had the Tuatha."

The image of a young Bres alone and afraid in the dark came to my mind, and I wanted to reach out and comfort him. "I still don't understand. Your family is part Tuatha, aren't they?"

He flicked his gaze to me, shadows darkening his eyes. "Yes. And we know more than most what they're capable of."

A chill ran through me, and I wrapped my arms around my midriff as if that might somehow protect me from the insanity of the situation. I wanted to be angry, defiant. I had no part in some stupid feud that had happened millennia ago, and I didn't want to be dragged into it now.

"What do you want from me?" I whispered.

Bres glanced up at the rear-view mirror and changed gears, taking a bend in the road too fast. "You're the Guardian. You can seal off the gateway once and for all. There should never have been a link left open. If they'd had enough power, there'd never have been a need for a Guardian, no possibility of the Tuatha returning."

I gave a bitter laugh. "Sure. Hang on until I wave my magic wand and close it for you."

His lips quirked up. "I don't think your Guardian status comes with a magic wand. But there is a ritual. The group I work with has the details. All I need is for you to say yes."

"You better not tell me I have to sacrifice a chicken while dancing naked under the light of the moon, or I'm out of here."

"Nothing quite that exciting ... unfortunately." He gave me a cheeky wink and my face heated.

Bres glanced in the rear-view mirror again and frowned, all playfulness leaving his expression.

"What is it?"

"We're being followed." Without warning, he pressed hard on the accelerator, causing me to let an involuntary yelp.

Alarm shot through me. "By who?"

"The Watchers of Danu, if I had to guess."

He took a sharp bend at such speed that he only just managed to right the car before it veered into the ditch that bordered the road.

I grabbed the "oh shit" handle with white knuckles. "How do you know they're following us? Maybe it's just someone out for a Sunday drive."

We were still on the country roads that led away from the old church, so it wasn't like there was anywhere else for a car to go. Surely it was just coincidence that there was a car behind us.

"They speed up whenever I do and their plates are blacked out. They're definitely following us. Hold on. I'm going to try to lose them."

Lose them? There was nowhere to bloody go!

Bres jerked the wheel to the right, and this time I did screech as the car turned onto a dirt road so narrow I hadn't even spotted it between the hedges. Every bone in my body rattled as we bounced over the rough terrain and branches scraped against the sides of the car.

I craned my neck around to look behind me. For a moment, the lane – if it could even be called that – was clear. Then suddenly, a silver car skidded into view behind us.

Shit. He was right; someone definitely was following us.

I mentally willed Bres to drive faster, but it was clear the terrain we were on had never been meant for normal cars. The silver car seemed to fare better than the BMW, however, and even as I watched, it began to close the distance between us.

Once more, Bres spun the wheel right, sending us careening through a row of bushes and into a field that was bordered on all sides by trees and hedging. Though the soft grass provided a much more comfortable ride than the stony lane, I couldn't help but wonder how the hell this would get us away from the other car.

As if in answer to my unspoken question, Bres did a U-turn and turned us back on ourselves. The silver car was just turning to follow us into the field as he did, and we narrowly missed it as he manoeuvred us back onto the narrow lane.

My heart was thundering as the branches once more tore at the doors and windows and something clunked against the underside of the car. How far were we from the nearest village? Would they leave us alone if we got somewhere more populated?

Yeah, sure. Like it had really made such a difference when they'd tried to kidnap me in the middle of a packed pub.

We emerged from the dirt track back onto the country road with a squeal of brakes and a hissed curse from Bres.

"Should I call the police?" I asked, fumbling in my pocket for my mobile.

"I can lose them. We just need to get off this stupid –"

His words were cut off as the silver car crashed through the bushes and slammed into the side of our car. The world started spinning, and I was distantly aware of someone – me? – screaming.

The car careened through the bushes on the far side of the road and the ground disappeared from beneath us. The next thing I knew, I was weightless and the world was suddenly the wrong way up.

It was a strange feeling. For a moment it almost seemed like someone had pressed pause on a film, and my brain registered a single thought: *This is going to hurt.*

We hit the ground with an explosive bang, and blinding pain became the only thing I knew.

I blinked my eyes open, a red haze of agony filling my vision. Something dug into my shoulder with bruising force and my left arm felt like it was on fire. It took a moment for my vision to clear and for me to realise I was still in the car. But why was everything upside down?

Someone called my name with an urgency that suggested it wasn't their first time trying to get my attention. I turned my head around with a groan and found Bres in the driver's seat next to me. Blood coated the side of his head and his skin was worryingly pale, but his eyes were open and alert.

"Aisling," he repeated, more insistent this time. "You need to get out of here. They'll be coming."

I blinked dumbly at him, trying to process his words. *Who'll be coming?*

As I tried to clear the fog from my head, he reached over. His sleeve rode up as he did, and I had only a moment to notice the tattoo of an oddly decorated "F" on his forearm before I heard a sharp click and the pressure against my shoulder disappeared.

Gravity got the last laugh as once again I fell, this time dropping to the roof of the car in a tangle of limbs. I hissed as a flare of pain shot through my shoulder.

"Shit, sorry. Are you okay?"

"Just dandy." I glared at him.

With difficulty, I twisted my body around in the small space so that I could get a better look at his injuries. I was numbly aware of voices in the distance and panic threatened to overwhelm me should I dare even acknowledge the insanity of my situation, so I focused on the practicalities.

"Can you move?" I asked him, hoping that the crumpled dashboard pressed against his body just looked worse than it was.

He shook his head with a grimace. "My leg is trapped. You have to leave me. It's you they want."

I ignored his order. Instead, I reached for the handle of the passenger side door and pushed. It moved an inch but then jammed. I growled in frustration and shoved harder, my shoulder screaming in protest.

With a groan of metal, the door gave way, sending me tumbling out onto the ground. I scrambled to my feet, numbly noting that the car had tumbled down a hill and only barely missed crashing into the nearby trees.

"Over here. They're over here!"

At the sound of a man's yell, the panic that I'd been trying hard to keep in check tightened around my chest like a band of steel. I stumbled around to the driver's side of the car and crouched down to yank fruitlessly at Bres's door.

"Go," he mouthed to me through the cracked window, his expression pleading.

Tears burned the back of my eyes as I looked hopelessly at the door that wouldn't budge and the dashboard beyond that had him pinned in place. Even if I could get to him, would I do more damage by moving him?

The pounding of footsteps grew louder behind me, and I knew I was out of time.

Desperation choked me as I reached out to him. He just nodded, his blue eyes calm and accepting.

And with that image burned into my mind, I turned and ran, almost tripping over my own feet as I blundered down the hill, tears blurring my vision.

The shadows consumed me as I reached the tree-line and ran blindly for cover. *Oh god, what had I done? I just left him back there, trapped and defenceless.*

Still, I ran until my lungs raged with a fire hot enough to compete with the agony in my shoulder, and I couldn't draw breath to run anymore. Twigs snapped beneath my weight and roots clawed at my feet, seemingly determined to trip me up. I was too afraid to look behind me, too afraid to see my pursuer close what little distance I'd put between myself and them.

Finally, I could run no more. My muscles refused any order I gave them to move and my legs buckled, sending me crashing to my knees. I choked back a sob.

No large, monstrous hand landed on my shoulder. No bogeyman jumped out at me from the shadows. So, after a tense moment of waiting, I finally looked around. The woods were empty. The only sound came from the rustling of the leaves in the breeze and my laboured breathing. They hadn't followed me.

Instead of making me feel better, that realisation caused a sickening feeling in the pit of my stomach. If they hadn't followed me, that could only mean one thing...

Bres!

Exhaustion immediately forgotten, I pushed to my feet. My muscles groaned in protest, but my legs held my weight. I forced myself to move slowly and with more thought as I wove a path through the trees, seeking a circuitous route back to the car. All the while, my eyes darted left and right, convinced I'd get caught at any second.

As I moved, I patted my now empty pocket. When had I last seen my phone? I'd definitely had it before the accident, so it must have fallen out in the car. If I could just make it back without being seen, maybe I could call for help – like I should have done to start with.

The surrounding shadows lessened and my breath hitched as I realised I'd reached the edge of the tree-line. I shifted so that I was behind a large tree and tentatively peered around the trunk.

From my position, I could make out the overturned car on the far side of the trees, but I couldn't see anyone around it. Feeling sick with fear, I crouched down low and edged away from my hiding place, hurrying towards the car.

No one tackled me to the ground as I moved or sounded the alarm at my approach. I could barely believe my luck when I made it to the wrecked BMW in one piece. Heart thundering, I bent down to peer through the driver's window.

The car was empty.

CHAPTER TEN

"The Watchers of Danu, you say? And they're what? Some kind of cult?" Sergeant Daniels asked me.

I hissed as the paramedic that was fussing around me dabbed at a cut I hadn't even noticed on my face. The pain in my left shoulder had eased only a little now that it was supported by a sling. The female paramedic checking me over didn't think anything was broken but was still none too pleased when I ignored her recommendation to let them take me to A&E for an x-ray.

I refused to leave the crash site, not while Bres was still missing. So, instead, I sat helpless in the back of an ambulance, answering the same stupid questions again and again.

"Does it really matter?" I snapped, biting back a scream of frustration. "They ran us off the road, and now my friend is missing. Surely that's reason enough for you to investigate?"

Sergeant Daniels, a stout man a few hairs shy of bald, ignored my outburst and continued to scribble in that stupid little notebook of his. It was clear that he thought I was crazy. Imaginary friends, strange cults, and car chases. Hell, I wasn't far from that assumption myself.

"We have people examining the scene now," he assured me in that same non-committal way he had every other time I'd pushed. "But any information you can give me about your friend or the" – a glance at his notes – "Watchers of Danu will help us greatly."

"I've already told you everything I know. Please, Bres is injured. We need to find him."

"We're doing everything we can, Ms. O'Meara." He flipped his notepad closed and looked in question at the paramedic, who pulled off her latex gloves with a nod. "Why don't I get one of our officers to escort you home?"

I stared at him in disbelief. "That's it? My friend is missing and you're just going to send me home?"

"There's nothing more you can do here. If you refuse to go to the hospital to get your shoulder checked out, then it would be best you go home and rest. You've been through a lot, and we may need to speak to you again."

He turned away from me, clearly deciding the matter was settled, and went to speak to a spotty-faced Garda who barely looked old enough to be out of school, let alone wearing a uniform. I ignored the gestures in my direction as I worried at my lip and tried to figure out what the hell to do.

Bres's overturned BMW was still being processed by the Gardaí and a tall woman with ginger hair caught my attention, though I couldn't say what made me notice her. Maybe the fact she was the only female officer on the scene?

She had her head bowed and was deep in conversation with a stocky bald man who stood with his back to me. It was only when they both shifted position that I got a view of his face.

I froze.

It was him. It was the guy who'd attacked me in the bar. And he was wearing a fucking police uniform.

My breath hitched and adrenaline spiked through me as I realised what an idiot I'd been. I'd just assumed I was safe once I'd found my phone in the wreckage and called the police.

I pushed myself up from where I was sitting on the edge of the ambulance and hurried over to Sergeant Daniels and the pimple-faced Garda, never once taking my eyes off the man and woman.

"Sergeant Daniels." Touching his elbow to get his attention, I tried hard to keep the edge of panic out of my voice. "I think you're right. I'd like to go home and get some rest, if that's okay?"

He watched me closely for a long minute before finally nodding. "Officer Reynolds here will take you."

I gave what I hoped was a grateful smile and indicated for Reynolds to lead the way. Every clipped step I took away from the wreckage ramped up the fear coursing through me. Any minute now the man would spot me.

But no one called after us, and I all but collapsed with relief as I got into the back of the police car and we pulled away from the scene.

My phone buzzed, making me jump. My hand shook as I pulled it out of my pocket only to see a message from Teagan asking if I was okay, that she was worried about me. It said a lot about my life that I stared at the phone in confusion for a good five minutes before I realised she was talking about my run-in with Pete the night before. The little white lie seemed so insignificant now compared to everything else that had happened.

After what seemed like an age, Officer Reynolds pulled the car to a stop outside the gates to Teagan's apartment building and turned to me with a smile. "Will you be okay by yourself?"

I opened my mouth to explain that I was staying with a friend, but stopped as I caught sight of his hand resting on the steering wheel. His sleeve had ridden up when he turned towards me, and I could just make out the edge of a colourful tattoo on the back of his forearm. I nodded mutely in answer to his question and climbed out of the car, my head whirring at the memory the sight triggered.

I waited until the police car disappeared in the

distance, then turned and made my way to the underground car park where my own car sat neglected. Teagan would probably be wondering where I was, but I didn't think strolling into the apartment looking like I'd just been in a car crash was a good idea. And this couldn't wait.

My shoulder protested with every gear change I made, but thankfully, traffic was light, and it didn't take me long to make my way to Smith & Mercer. I found a questionably legal parking spot around the corner from the offices and checked myself in the rear-view mirror.

The cuts and scrapes on my face didn't look too bad now that the blood had been cleared away. A nice purplish bruise had bloomed on one side of my forehead, but a bit of messing with my hair more or less covered that up. If anyone bothered to look at me properly, they'd think I'd been dragged through a hedge backwards, but I was counting on anyone I met to be too absorbed by their own problems to ask questions.

You'd think that the offices would be closed given it was late on a Sunday afternoon. However, the law firm thoughtfully ensured that employees had access to their work seven days a week, just in case they had nothing better to do with their weekend.

Dave, the security guard, looked up with raised eyebrows as I entered the building, my head angled as best I could to hide the signs of the crash. "Hey, Aisling. What has you in on a Sunday?"

I gave a martyred sigh. "Clifford forgot something. He asked me to get it for him."

Dave tutted and shook his head, knowing all too well that my boss wouldn't think twice about disturbing someone else's weekend to have them play fetch for him. He waved me on and I hurried to the elevator, blowing out a shaky breath when the stainless steel doors closed.

The offices were empty except for one very haggard-looking paralegal, who glanced up only long enough to acknowledge my presence before returning to whatever had her chewing her pencil to a nub. I was careful to keep my pace casual as I made my way to my desk, palms sweaty with the knowledge that what I was about to do could get me fired in a heartbeat.

I tapped my foot impatiently as the computer loaded up ever so slowly. With a furtive glance over my shoulder, just to be certain my boss hadn't magically appeared, I typed in Clifford's username.

Technically, I shouldn't know my boss's password. In a legal firm, it was vital that our IT security was airtight – particularly when it came to confidential files held by the partners. But I could hardly be blamed if Clifford was so unimaginative that he'd chosen "Password123" as his password.

Sure enough, when I typed it in and hit enter, my boss's desktop loaded up. I cringed at the hoard of icons strewn haphazardly around the screen. How could anyone work like this? It was no surprise really that he was so disorganised.

Returning to the task at hand, I grabbed the stack of folders from my "to be filed" tray. It didn't take me long to find the one I was looking for, and my stomach churned at the sight of the decorative "F" on the cover.

In all the chaos, I thought maybe my imagination had been playing tricks on me, but no, there it was, the same image that Bres had tattooed on his forearm.

I hadn't thought much about the mysterious unnamed client since Clifford had confirmed that we won the contract; I had better things to worry about in my life than clients that over-valued their own self-importance. Now, though, this file contained information that could help me find Bres. So, they could shove their client confidentiality up their arse.

Holding my breath, I typed the client code into the search bar. A single file popped up and I didn't hesitate before opening it. The title jumped off the screen at me, and my breath left me in a whoosh.

The Order of the Fomori.

I scrubbed a hand over my face and leaned back in the chair. There was no way this was a coincidence. Bres had told me that his heritage was part Tuatha, part Fomorian. Given his obvious disdain for the Tuatha, it was logical to assume his allegiance lay with the latter, but he'd never mentioned anything about an order.

Or had he?

He had used "we" more than once. I'd just assumed he'd meant it in an abstract way. It didn't matter now, though. I needed help, and this was the only way I could think of to get it.

I grabbed the notepad that rested next to my keyboard and wrote down the address listed on the file. It was time I met our new client.

CHAPTER ELEVEN

I had a dreamless sleep for the first time in as long as I could remember. Though every fibre of my being demanded that I help Bres, exhaustion won out shortly after my trip to Smith & Mercer.

I'd gotten behind the wheel of my car, determined to pay a visit to the Order of the Fomori, but when I'd pulled out into traffic and narrowly avoided a collision with a forty-foot truck, I'd finally had to accept my limitations.

Teagan was out when I'd gotten back to the apartment, and the relief I felt made me hate myself even more. When I found a giant bag of Doritos with a note saying there was Ben & Jerry's ice cream in the freezer too, should I need it, my guilt intensified so much that I almost choked on it.

The long, scalding shower had been both torture and bliss, and I'd barely managed to keep my eyes open before falling into bed. If Teagan came to check on me when she got home, I had no idea, as oblivion took me in seconds.

The first thing I did upon waking was check my phone in the desperate hope that there would be a message from the police to say they'd found Bres. Or better yet, a message from Bres himself. There had been neither.

The second thing I did was call in sick to work.

Dressing as quickly as I could, I slipped out of the apartment once more. I typed the address I'd taken from Clifford's files into Google Maps and cursed every single car on the road as I crawled my way through rush hour traffic.

Number 7 King's Street was not what I expected. The nondescript grey building showed little signs of life from the outside, with no windows to indicate what lay behind the brick facade. A mahogany door was the only entry, and a small brass plaque on the wall beside it informed me I was at the Museum of Irish Antiquities.

I eyed the plaque suspiciously. A quick Google this morning had turned up nothing on the Order of the Fomori. This was definitely the address that Clifford had listed in the file, but what would the Order have to do with a museum?

I pushed open the door and was instantly swallowed by the dimly lit interior. A mahogany desk waited unmanned just inside the door, ornate candelabras framing it on either side. Behind the reception stood a pair of frosted glass doors that I assumed led into the museum itself, and a few cursory pamphlets had been laid out on a small coffee table that was bordered on either side by wing-backed chairs.

There was no sign of a receptionist, or of those annoying little bells that I always felt rude using to call one. And since there was also no sign of a price list for entry I decided to go find someone myself rather than waiting around to be noticed.

I pushed open the glass door and peered into the narrow room beyond. The first thing that struck me was the musty smell that tickled my nose and left me with a sudden urge to sneeze. Each side of the room was lined with glass cases, and spotlights directed the focus to the objects that lay within. Curious, I made my way over to the one closest to me and peered through the glass.

A book rested on a bed of soft green velvet. Its leather exterior was cracked and worn, and though I was no expert, it definitely looked old to me. The title was faded but still legible, its letters crafted in beautiful swirls on the cover in a language that looked like it might have been Gaeilge, or at least some old form of it. A small white card below the book declared it to be "Éire, an Ancient Mythology & History, author unknown".

I wondered idly if it held any stories about the Tuatha Dé Danann and the Fomorians, and if so, would they corroborate the stories I'd found online, or the ones Bres had told me?

Next to the book sat a small stone with unusual

marks carved into its surface. A shiver ran down my spine as I pictured a much larger version of the stone that I'd seen only the day before back at the Church of the Blessed Heart.

"Ms. O'Meara?"

I jumped and let out a squeak of surprise. Turning, I found a man standing behind me. A slight frown marred his wrinkled face as he observed me with a stiff posture and hands clasped behind his back. The black and gold trim double-breasted suit he wore suggested that he was the museum curator, but it was the black eye patch covering his left eye that kept drawing my attention.

"I'm sorry, I didn't –" I cut off suddenly as his words registered through my initial surprise. "How do you know my name?"

"Oh, we know all about you." And with that cryptic comment, he turned and headed deeper into the museum.

For a minute, I just watched, dumbfounded. Then I hurried to catch up, following like the obedient dog he clearly expected me to be. If playing nice helped me get Bres back safe and sound, then I'd bite my tongue. For now.

As we made our way further into the building, the glass cases were replaced by paintings and tapestries of varying sizes and shapes. Most of them depicted grand battle scenes, and the colours were so vibrant that I had difficulty believing them to be antiques.

"Some of these pieces of art date back over three

millennia," the curator commented, almost as if he'd read my thoughts.

I raised a sceptical eyebrow but kept my mouth shut; I wasn't here to debate the historical merit of the museum's exhibits. Instead, I asked, "Where are we going?"

Silence was my only reply.

The logical voice in the back of my head pointed out that following a man whose name I didn't even know, to a location that he refused to disclose, was probably a bad idea. In fact, it sounded like the start of a b-rated horror movie script.

I was just about to draw the line when we turned a corner and came to a dead end. The small space was empty except for a large tapestry adorning the wall. Something about the image it depicted sent a shiver of recognition through me.

Instead of the usual epic battles I'd grown accustomed to seeing on the walls, this tapestry showed a celebration of sorts. A man and woman stood facing each other in the centre of it all, and a young boy with blond hair sat at their feet. The boy's piercing blue eyes drew me in, and it took me a moment to tear my eyes away long enough to examine the rest of the image.

My mouth went dry.

I hadn't noticed it at first glance because of the side profiles, but the woman's strawberry blonde hair was so richly coloured that I took a second look. It was her. The woman from my dreams.

The curator stepped up to the tapestry, either oblivious to, or unconcerned by, my inner turmoil. He moved a corner of it aside to reveal a keypad on the wall beneath it. Careful to conceal his movements from me, he typed something into it before drawing the tapestry back completely to reveal a door.

A soft click sounded and a decorative "F" glowed on the door for a moment before fading. He pushed open the door and indicated for me to proceed into the long corridor beyond.

My feet were moving before I could consider the sanity of my actions. Unease skittered through me, and I was in no way reassured by the curator's stony expression as I passed him.

The wine-coloured carpet was soft beneath my feet and wood panelling lined the walls on either side. Brass sconces lit the way, and a wooden door waited at the end of the hallway. I didn't bother asking questions as we made our way towards it, since they'd no doubt be ignored anyway.

The curator took a large brass key from his pocket and unlocked the second door – no fancy keypads for this one – to reveal a large lobby like you might expect to find in a plush hotel. There was a stone fireplace against one wall, and winged armchairs were scattered in clusters around the room, some of which were occupied. The hushed conversations trailed off as the men seated in them turned to look at us.

All eyes followed us as we traversed the room to the next hallway. This one was similar to the first, but had unmarked doors on either side. Were they bedrooms?

Offices? What kind of place was this, because it sure as shit wasn't just a museum?

Finally, we came to a stop in front of a pair of mahogany doors. The curator rapped briskly.

"Enter," came a man's equally brisk response.

The curator pushed open one of the doors and moved aside to allow me to pass. The room beyond looked like the offices of many of the CEOs I'd encountered in my professional life. Rich wood furnishings tastefully complemented the accents of black and polished silver, and a large bookcase ran across the rear wall of the room.

The man sitting behind the mahogany desk had black hair lightly dusted with grey, and I pegged him as being in his late fifties, maybe. He watched me with piercing grey eyes that gave little away. I didn't know why, but I disliked him instantly.

"You can leave us, Bill," he said to the curator without looking at the man.

The door closed behind me with a click and my whole body tensed. There was no sound of a lock turning, however, so I forced myself to relax and at least feign some degree of confidence.

An awkward silence settled between us, and I recognised it for the power play that it was. I hadn't been offered a seat, but I was perfectly happy to stand. I didn't plan on being here long, and I wasn't going to waste time on these stupid mind games.

"I'm looking for the Order of the Fomori."

If I'd been hoping for a reaction to the words, I was

sorely disappointed. The man's expression didn't change; he didn't even flinch at the name.

"What business do you have with the Order?"

"None, if I could help it," I muttered under my breath. I squared my shoulders and looked him dead in the eye. "The Watchers of Danu have taken Bres."

CHAPTER TWELVE

I wasn't sure exactly what kind of reaction I was expecting. Shock? Outrage? Concern? I didn't get any of those from the pompous git sitting behind his fancy desk in his fancy office. I got nothing.

"Did you hear what I said?" Maybe I hadn't actually said the words out loud? I'd debated what I might say the whole way here, so maybe I'd said it in my head again. "They've taken Bres."

"I heard you, Ms. O'Meara."

I bristled. The other man – Bill – had known my name too. Crossing my arms, I glared at him.

"Maybe you'd mind telling me exactly how it is you know my name? It seems rather unfair considering you haven't bothered to offer me yours."

The smile he gave me failed to reach his eyes as he inclined his head in acknowledgement. "Forgive my rudeness. My name is Declan Bannon, and the man that brought you here is William Murphy, our ... museum curator."

Well, that explained nothing.

I refocused on the reason I was here, deciding that it didn't matter who the hell I was speaking to so long as they helped me. "The police aren't doing anything to find Bres. The Order needs to help him."

Bannon leaned back in his chair and steepled his fingers. "What would our help be worth?"

I blinked, momentarily taken aback. "What do you mean? Bres is one of you. I know he is. I saw his tattoo. You can't seriously be saying that you'd just leave him out there."

"Bres knew the risks associated with his work."

Anger flared through me as I took in his unmoved expression. I knew people like him. I'd sat across a boardroom table from enough of them at Smith & Mercer. People like him only cared about one thing: what was in it for them.

I gritted my teeth, stubbornness warring with the growing desperation to find Bres. He was in this mess because he tried to help me. I couldn't just turn my back on him again, even if the Order were clearly so willing to.

"I'll do the ritual. That's what you want, isn't it? Find Bres and I'll complete the ritual to stop the Tuatha Dé Danann from returning."

Bannon was quiet for so long that a terrified part of me wondered if he'd actually refuse. Finally, he smiled, a chilling smile that told me with a sense of dread that I'd played right into his hands.

"Deal."

He stood from the desk and strode to the bookcase behind him. He pulled out a book, seemingly at random, and revealed a small keypad similar to the one I'd seen behind the tapestry. I was about to point out just how clichéd it was to have a secret passage when he keyed something into the pad and the bookcase slid back. The words died on my lips as a square room with stainless steel walls appeared.

"Come with me," he ordered, stopping just shy of clicking his fingers.

The room was a complete antithesis of everything I'd seen of the building so far. Where the décor up to this point had screamed old-school money, this was sterile and clinical. One complete side of the room was covered in monitors and boasted an IT set-up that would probably be any hacker's wet dream.

"Computers are the magic of the modern day," Bannon said, clearly noticing my surprise. "Those who fail to embrace the new forms of magic deserve to be left in the past."

As if to highlight his point, he moved to one of the computers and typed rapidly on the keyboard. A soft beep sounded and the stainless steel walls began to slide away, revealing glass cases on the two remaining walls. LED lights illuminated the objects within, and I stared at them in awe.

A spear, a sword, and a small cast-iron pot had been carefully arranged on one side of the room, and the other was covered in ancient-looking scrolls and chunks of stone carved with strange markings. Teagan probably would have understood the historical relevance of the items better than I did, but somehow I knew that despite their well-preserved appearance, they were very old.

More typing sounded and there was another beep before a section in the centre of the floor began to slide away. Even though I was nowhere near it, I stepped back in surprise as a cylindrical glass case rose from the floor. Inside, a book bound in cracked brown leather rested next to a small box on a satin covered podium.

Bannon turned to me, his grey eyes as hard as the steel that had moments ago surrounded us. "That book holds the ritual you must complete. I'm not a heartless man, Ms. O'Meara, but this cause is too great to allow emotions to interfere. So, let me make this perfectly clear – if you betray us, I will see to it that Bres pays the price."

I swallowed hard, no doubt in my mind that he meant it.

"What do I need to do?"

Teagan was waiting for me when I got home. She stood and looked at me in silence, taking in the scrapes on my face and the way I was cradling my now aching left arm. Her expression was tight, with anger or concern I couldn't tell, but I could feel the barely coiled tension in the room.

"The police called wanting to speak to you."

"Did they find Bres?" I blurted out, a tiny seed of hope blossoming in my chest.

"Who's Bres? What is going on, Aisling?" She slumped down onto the sofa, something like hurt flashing across her face. "First you bail on me on Saturday, then you avoid me all day yesterday, and now I have to find out from the police that you've been in an accident."

I grimaced, realising how bad it must look from her side. I hadn't purposely tried to keep her in the dark. I just didn't know how to explain it all without sounding crazy. And right now, the thing that mattered most was getting Bres back safely.

"I'm sorry, I didn't mean for you to find out this way. It's just been a very weird few days. Did the police say anything about Bres?" I asked again, trying to keep the desperation out of my voice.

Teagan tilted her head and assessed me with a curious glint in her eye. "You're seeing someone new," she said after a moment. "That was why it freaked you out so much, running into Pete the other night."

I glared at her, my patience wearing thin.

She sighed in defeat. "No, they didn't mention anyone called Bres. They just wanted to ask you a few more questions about the accident. What the hell happened? You look like shit."

The tiny kernel of hope I'd felt died, and I didn't even have the energy to feel insulted by her observation. The bag I carried over my good shoulder suddenly felt a lot heavier, as if reminding me of the responsibility I carried.

"Someone ran us off the road. My shoulder is sore, but they don't think anything's broken. Bres got trapped in the car. I went for help, but when I came back, he was gone."

My voice cracked as the lie burned my throat. I hadn't gone for help; I'd run away like a scared little girl. Well, I wasn't going to run away this time. I'd do what needed to be done, and I'd damn well make sure that Declan Bannon kept up his side of the bargain.

Teagan reached out and squeezed my hand. "What can I do to help?"

Her concern just made me feel worse, so I gently pulled my hand away and attempted a small smile. "The police are doing everything they can. I think I just need to rest."

She didn't say anything, but I could feel her worried gaze on me as I made my way to the bedroom.

I closed the door behind me and slumped against it. Part of me wanted nothing more than to curl up into a ball and cry, but it wouldn't change anything. So, I set the bag down carefully on my bed and opened it to reveal the box and book inside.

Dawn of the summer solstice was less than twelve hours away. I needed to rest if I was going to be ready, but the thought of closing my eyes filled me with dread. What would happen to Bres if I screwed this up?

My eyelids grew heavy as the weight of the day pressed against me, and with a resigned sigh, I undressed and climbed under the cool sheets.

I flicked the book open to the page that Bannon had marked and scanned the words. The language looked similar to the other book I'd noted in the museum – some old form of Gaeilge that might as well have been Arabic for all that I recognised it. Luckily, someone had folded a small sheet of paper inside the book that contained the phonetic pronunciation of the words.

Bannon had made me memorise the steps of the ritual before leaving the Order. They'd played over and over in my head the entire way back to the apartment, yet I still had a panicked feeling that I'd blank when the time came. So, I read and I read them again. But eventually, I couldn't fight the clawing hands of sleep from pulling me under.

Whether the aroma of rosemary and lemongrass had become such a constant in my life that I no longer noticed it, or whether it was simply missing, I wasn't sure. What I did know was that I once again stood in the clearing, surrounded by the large standing stones.

The woman with strawberry blonde hair – the one from the tapestry – was there again. She wasn't paying any attention to me, however. She stood in a circle with six other men and women, her determined gaze focusing straight ahead.

On the perimeter of the standing stones, a larger circle had been formed. Faceless men and women tightly gripped hands in an unbroken chain. The chanting hadn't started yet, though I knew it was only a matter of time.

Energy crackled in the air and along my skin. Despite the cloudless sky above, there was a heaviness, like a storm was brewing. Tendrils of red filled the eastern horizon as the morning sun broke free of its nightly constraints.

Dawn, I realised.

With the first rays of light, the chanting started. It came from the outside circle in a low and steady tempo. Within the circle, the seven figures bent to pick something up from the ground in front of them. They straightened in unison, a terrifying look of resolve mirrored in each of their expressions.

Each grasping their respective objects, the inner circle began their own chant. The cadence was different from the chant I'd heard every other time before, and though I couldn't understand the words, I could *feel* the intent behind them.

The energy shifted in the circle. A wind that hadn't existed only moments ago rustled the grass and blew tendrils of hair into my eyes. I spun in a slow circle, only now realising that I was standing in the very centre of whatever was happening.

The power grew, and every fibre of my being rebelled, alarm bells sounding in my head as my instincts demanded that I run.

At last, the woman from the tapestry looked at me. The sorrow and regret I saw on her face was achingly familiar; I'd seen it in my dreams many times now.

Holding my gaze, she drew a jagged blade from the emerald green sash wrapped around her waist. Slowly, she ran the blade down her forearm. Vibrant red blood oozed up from the incision.

She angled her arm towards the ground and a bead of blood ran down her forearm to drop to the earth at her feet. Then, she offered the dagger to the man standing on her right.

He followed her lead, as did the person after that, and the one after that, until all seven had committed their blood to the earth.

An eerie howl sounded and the wind whipped up into a vortex within the circle. It roared so loudly that I couldn't tell whether or not they were still chanting. My vision blurred and it felt like I, too, was spinning.

I spun and spun and spun. Then there was just silence.

The world stopped turning, and the energy disappeared. I stood alone at the centre of the standing stones, the circle of seven now little more than my imagination. And the ground outside the stones was littered with bodies.

CHAPTER THIRTEEN

Remnants of my dream followed me into my waking hours and a deep-seated sense of unease lingered as I made my way back to the Church of the Blessed Heart. Dawn was still an hour away and the roads were eerily quiet as I drove. The book and box rested on the passenger seat next to me, and though I knew it had to be my imagination playing tricks on me, I could've sworn they were vibrating with energy.

I'd woken from my uneasy sleep with the book splayed open on my chest. Whether the figurative and literal weight of its presence had contributed to the dream's horrifying new finale, I wasn't sure. All I knew was that I was more than ready to resign my role as Guardian and get back to my normal life – even if it had seemed completely messed up only a couple of weeks ago. It was funny how perspectives could change in such a short time.

I pulled the car to a stop in one of the narrow lay-bys and killed the engine. A deafening silence fell, broken only by the pounding of my heart. For a long moment, I just sat there staring at the objects on my passenger seat. They looked so innocuous that it was almost laughable to believe they scared me so much. But they did.

Come on, I chastised myself. *The sooner you do this, the sooner it'll all be over.* Before I could second-guess myself, I grabbed the book and box and climbed out of the car.

The walk from the arched oak trees through the graveyard was shorter than I remembered. I'd always imagined it would be creepy to be in a graveyard in the dark, but there was something oddly peaceful about the way the waning moon highlighted the tombstones of those at rest. It was the seemingly empty field beyond the church that made me want to run screaming.

Even though I'd seen past the illusion, there was no sign of the standing stone circle while I remained on this side of the boundary. I couldn't even spot the strange shimmer that had been present in the air when I'd stood within the circle and looked back at Bres only a couple of days before.

The tissue with the handful of soil rested in my pocket. Some part of me had known I'd need it again, but I honestly hadn't believed it would be this soon.

Almost in autopilot, I climbed over the low stone wall and made my way into the field, stopping just before the area of raised ground. I reached into my pocket for the tissue, but my hands were trembling so much that I fumbled and dropped the book from my other hand.

It landed open on the ground, displaying a page that I'd seen the night before in my brief perusal of the book. I'd felt a strange draw to it then, and I felt that same pull now, but I had no idea what the odd words and symbols on the page meant.

The sound of a car engine broke through my reverie, and I froze for a heartbeat.

A quick glance around showed me a glimmer of headlights approaching from the distance, and any hope I had that the car was going the opposite way was quickly squashed. The Church of the Blessed Heart was in the middle of nowhere, and I couldn't think of a reason anyone else would be out here before dawn. Unless...

Spurred into action, I grabbed the book from where it had fallen on the ground, all thought of the open page forgotten as I slammed it shut. I'd just tugged the tissue of dirt from my pocket when the purr of the car's engine abruptly cut off.

The slamming of a car door broke the heavy silence of the morning. I was running out of time.

I didn't stop to think. I just shook the soil into my hand, scrunched my eyes closed, and took the final step to bring me across the illusion's boundary.

The reddish-purple hue of the approaching dawn

provided an ominous backdrop as the circle of standing stones came into view once more. My chest tightened in panic at the sight of them as memories of my dream resurfaced.

The charred earth was the only remnant of the ritual that had been performed here, but it was enough to remind me of the dead bodies that had littered the ground, and the lives that had clearly been sacrificed.

Footsteps crunched nearby, and I jerked my head back in time to spot a man and woman climbing over the low wall that bordered the field. Though there was limited light this far out in the countryside, I recognised them both instantly.

The stocky bald man who had tried to abduct me from the pub took the lead as the ginger-haired police-woman who'd been with him at the crash scene followed. The Watchers of Danu had found me.

My heart thundered as they grew closer. I knew I couldn't see through the illusion when I'd been on the other side of the spell, but could they? If they had some of the soil, it wouldn't matter, anyway; they could be in the circle with me in seconds.

The man's foot caught on something and he muttered a low curse as he tripped. His female companion silenced him with a glare.

"Quit your whining. If you'd approached her the way I'd suggested, we wouldn't be in this situation," she snapped, irritation clear in her tone, even from a distance.

A huff conveyed the man's disagreement as he got to his feet and brushed himself off. "I told you, she's working for them. You're nuts if you think she'll see sense." He came to a stop and looked around. "Are you sure she's here?"

Ice chilled my veins as the woman turned and seemed to look straight at me.

"Oh, she's here."

Shit. Shit. Shit. What was I going to do?

I held my breath, afraid to move or even release the air in my lungs in case they heard it. Any moment now, she'd cross through the illusion and see me.

But she didn't. She made no attempt to move forward, just continued to look in my general direction with a thoughtful expression on her face.

Without taking my eyes from her or her partner, I lowered myself down to one knee. My hands shook as, ever so slowly, I placed the book and the box on the ground. I'd memorised the ritual and it should be simple enough once I didn't fuck up the pronunciation. Could I complete it before they found a way to stop me? Chewing on my lip, I carefully opened the book to the page I needed.

"Aisling," the woman called.

I jumped, nearly knocking over the box that rested on the ground beside me. With a panicked hiss, I grabbed for it.

A stillness came over the woman, like a predator that had just scented her prey. I closed my eyes and silently cursed my stupidity.

"We're not here to hurt you, Aisling. I promise, we just want to talk."

Despite the fear that was all but crippling me, I couldn't help my snort of disbelief. Did she seriously think I was going to buy that?

As if reading my thoughts, she grimaced. "My name's Siobhán. I know you got off to a bad start with the Watchers and I'd like to apologise for that." She flashed an irritated glare at the man standing to her left with his arms crossed. "Brian here's not exactly what you'd call a people person. He shouldn't have approached you the way he did on Saturday night."

Brian gaped at her in disbelief.

Neither of them had made an attempt to cross over the illusion's barrier, so I opened the box and lifted out the small bundle wrapped in green silk cloth. As I did, I casually commented, "Approached seems like a very nice word for attempted abduction."

Brian blanched at that and sputtered, "What are you talking about? I never tried to abduct you. I just wanted to talk to you and you had your goons from the Order attack me."

I let a harsh laugh as I unwrapped the cloth and spread the contents out on the ground. A lock of hair. A small stone with markings similar to those on the standing stone. A piece of blackened bark from a tree. A dented bronze coin. A milky white crystal. A ragged square of cloth, the design now faded beyond recognition. And finally, a small bundle of rosemary and lemongrass.

"Why would I have someone attack you? Do I look like the kind of person that has 'goons'?"

"Maybe because you're working with the Order and _"

Siobhán jabbed him in the ribs and he huffed out a breath, but stopped talking.

"Maybe leave the talking to me from now on," she snapped before turning her attention back to me. "We know you've been speaking to the Order, and we know the lies they've been telling you. We just want to give you the true story."

My hand stilled just as I reached for the sheet with the phonetic pronunciation of the ritual spell. There was that stupid word again. Everyone kept promising me the "truth". Well, they could all shove it where the sun doesn't shine.

"Sure. Why don't you tell me the real story then?"

Siobhán was silent for a moment. Whether surprised that I was being so cooperative, or getting her lies in order, I wasn't sure.

I didn't wait for her to get her bearings before I picked up the piece of paper and unfolded it. The words were still clear in my mind after memorising them the night before, but I scanned them one final time to be sure.

"The Order told you that the Tuatha were the bad guys, right?" Siobhán said finally. "That they were power hungry and wanted all the magic for themselves? What they told you was true, but it wasn't the

Tuatha who wanted to enslave the people of Ireland and keep the magic. It was the Fomorians."

I picked up the objects from the ground, and blocking her out, I began to whisper the words of the ritual as quietly as I could. The lock of hair I placed at the base of the first standing stone, the small stone at the second.

"The Tuatha Dé Danann are linked to this land and its magic," she continued, her words only vaguely piercing through my consciousness. "The Fomorians saw the power it gave them and they wanted it for themselves."

The bark of the tree I laid at the third standing stone, and the bronze coin at the fourth.

"They killed for that power –"

My steps faltered.

"And when that didn't work, they feigned a truce with the Tuatha. They intertwined their bloodline with ours in the hope that it would give them control of the magic."

I placed the crystal at the fifth stone, and the cloth at the sixth. Her words reverberated in my head, but I gritted my teeth and forced myself to focus only on the ritual.

"The truce didn't last, of course. The leaders of the Tuatha discovered that the Fomorians were seeking a way to claim full control of the magic for themselves."

She fell silent, and I froze in front of the seventh stone.

Nearly there. I just had to keep her talking a little longer. "What happened?"

She took a shaky breath. "They decided that the magic was too powerful to risk it falling under the control of the Fomorians. So, the Tuatha Dé Danann sacrificed themselves and their people to keep it safe."

CHAPTER FOURTEEN

Memories of my dreams assaulted me and I froze, inches away from placing the herbs at the final standing stone. Sacrificed themselves? Was that what I'd seen in my dream last night? I shook my head; that didn't make sense.

"If they sacrificed their entire race in some grand, noble gesture, how are you here? The Watchers of Danu are from the Tuatha Dé Danann bloodline, aren't they?"

"You're right." Siobhán inclined her head in acknowledgement. "Our ancestors were far enough removed from the heart of the magic that they survived the ritual and continued the bloodline. Any magic they did hold was lost to them, however. Your bloodline was the only exception, given that the role of the Guardian was built into the ritual."

"My bloodline?" I dropped the herbs into position and clenched my fist tight to stop the trembling.

The pause was so long that I looked up, wondering if Siobhán and Brian had actually left – not that I'd be so lucky.

"The Guardian bloodline," Siobhán said slowly, an edge of confusion evident in her tone. "It's as much a part of the Tuatha line as we are. Didn't you know that?"

"Some representative she is, considering she's so willing to consort with the enemy," Brian muttered just loud enough for me to hear, earning himself another warning glare from his partner.

Part of the Tuatha line? That wasn't right. Bres had told me that the Guardian came from the Fomorian bloodline. Why would he lie to me?

I moved back to the centre of the circle, my head spinning. All that remained was for me to add my blood, and the ritual would be complete. Still, her words settled in the pit of my stomach, a seed of doubt sprouting where resolve had been only moments before.

Gritting my teeth, I bent down and picked up the last object from the box: a jagged blade wrapped in an emerald green sash. The dagger looked exactly like the one I'd seen the woman use in my dream, and I'd have sworn the sash was the one the woman had worn. But that couldn't be the case. They'd have been ancient.

I ran my fingertips tentatively along the rough edge of the blade. Just one quick slice and this could all be over. Yet I hesitated.

"Why should I believe you?" I asked, eyes fixed on the dagger in my hand.

"I've no reason to lie to you," Siobhán replied with a shrug. "The Watchers of Danu exist for only one reason – to keep magic safe from the Order and ensure our ancestor's sacrifice wasn't in vain. You've had the visions. Surely you must feel the truth of what I'm saying."

That seed of doubt twisted in my gut. I gripped the dagger tighter.

Of course they were going to tell me they were the good guys. What bad guy ever came out and admitted to being in the wrong? I knew well enough from working in a law firm just how easy it was to twist words to suit your purpose.

But what was to stop the Order of the Fomori from doing the same thing?

I bit my lip. "If you want me to trust you, tell me where Bres is."

Brian and Siobhán gave each other a look that I couldn't interpret in the dim light before Siobhán turned back to me, something uncertain in her posture now.

"Bres is missing?"

It sounded like genuine surprise in Siobhán's voice, but how could that be? Were there people higher up in the Watchers of Danu pulling strings these two didn't know about?

"Your people followed us," I said, watching their

reactions closely. "They ran us off the road and they took him."

Siobhán shook her head vehemently. "That wasn't us. No one from the Watchers has been authorised to approach you since the fuck-up on Saturday night."

Brian crossed his arms, and I could have sworn he actually pouted at his error being highlighted yet again.

I scoffed. "So what, some other random group of people just so happened to start following me at the same time you approached me?"

"The Order of the Fomori has been keeping tabs on you ever since they discovered you were Guardian," Siobhán said. "They were the ones who attacked you on Saturday night – though for what purpose, I don't know. Brian tried to stop them and that's when Bres stepped in to play knight in shining armour. The Watchers of Danu have known who you were from the moment the role of Guardian passed to you, and we haven't interfered in your life."

"Until now," I pointed out.

"Until now," she conceded. "Once the Order discovered your identity, we knew we had to speak to you before they filled your head with lies."

Her words settled in the quiet between us, and that uncomfortable knot twisted again in my stomach. She sounded so logical and reasonable, but I didn't want reason. My life had been turned on its head ever since I'd stepped into this damned place. I just wanted it all to be over and for things to go back to normal.

I latched onto that anger, not willing to examine the uncomfortable thought that was niggling at the back of my mind, the what-if.

"You knew I was the Guardian the whole time and you didn't think to clue me in on all this?" My hand tightened around the dagger once more as all the fear and worry of the recent weeks bubbled up inside me. "You say you're on my side, yet you left me to find out about all of this by myself. You let me think I was going crazy."

The truth of my words filled the space between us. I was so sick of it all. I couldn't face the dreams again; I just wanted it to stop.

Without even thinking, I took the dagger and sliced down the inside of my forearm. Fire blazed up my arm and I hissed at the pain.

Siobhán and Brian both tensed.

"Aisling," Siobhán called in alarm. "What are you doing?"

I didn't answer her. I was too busy trying to breathe through the pain to think straight.

She held up her hands in a placating gesture, her attempts at sounding calm failing miserably. "You're right. We should have explained it all. But I swear to you, we had our reasons. For centuries, the history of the Guardian was passed down through your family line. The responsibility was a heavy burden, though, and one of your ancestors took her own life because it was too much for her to deal with. After that, it was decided that the Guardian wouldn't be told of her role unless it became completely necessary. The Watchers of Danu kept an eye on each new one that came, but they were left in peace to live their lives as much as possible."

As she hurried to justify the situation to me, I stared, mesmerised, at the blood that welled up on my forearm. A single drop was all that was needed. Just one drop and the dreams would stop.

Brian cut across Siobhán abruptly. "What did the Order promise you? They won't share the magic with you, I can guarantee that. They want it all for themselves, just like their ancestors did."

The magic? What the hell was he talking about?

"The leaders of a whole race were willing to give up their lives and the lives of their families because they were so afraid of what would happen if the Fomorians got their wish," he continued, his tone harsh and making no effort to be conciliatory. "What does that tell you?"

I tried to make sense of what he was saying, but my head was fuzzy with the pain that still radiated along my arm. "If they gave themselves up so willingly, why are they trying to find a way back now?" I called, my eyes flicking to the blood that was slowly running down my arm.

"What do you mean?" Siobhán asked.

"The dreams, the visions, whatever the hell they are. They've been messing with my head. Trying to convince me to open the gateway so that they can come back. Not much of a sacrifice if they only ever intended it to be temporary."

"Aisling, no, that's not what –"

I blocked out the panicked protests; I'd heard enough. This ended now.

I angled my arm down to the ground and focused on the single drop of blood that slid free of my skin. For a moment, nothing happened.

And then the world exploded.

CHAPTER FIFTEEN

Every cell in my body vibrated in time to the ringing in my ears. I was still in the centre of the stone circle, but something had changed. Jagged cracks ran down the centre of all seven standing stones, and the strange energy I had always felt in the place was just ... gone.

At some point the dawn had coaxed the sun from its resting place, and it was only when I noticed the blood red of the morning sky above me that I realised I was half sprawled on the ground. I looked around, dazed.

Had it worked? Had I closed the gateway?

My gaze stopped on two figures lying in the grass just beyond the boundary of the illusion spell. Siobhán and Brian. Neither of them were moving, and panic gripped me. Oh god, had I killed them?

I scrambled to my feet, just about to call out to them when movement near the old church caught my attention. A shadowy figure stepped out from the ruins, and I had to blink a few times to convince myself I wasn't imagining things.

Bres sauntered towards me. Safe and unharmed.

I moved to run to him, but something about his posture caused me to stop. He was smiling, but there was something cold about it that seemed alien on his normally playful expression. He gave only the briefest glance at the two prone bodies as he came to a stop beside them.

"You did it, Aisling," he said, putting his hands into the pockets of the jeans that hung loosely on his hips. "I wasn't sure you would, but you really came through in the end."

I watched him, uncertainty dulling my relief at seeing him unhurt. "You're okay. How did you…"

"How did I escape the Watchers of Danu? Oh, that was easy." His grin widened. "They never had me."

My throat went dry. A sickening feeling settled in the pit of my stomach, right where that seed had planted itself.

"Who?" I asked in a whisper.

He laughed and tutted in disappointment. "The Order, of course. The Watchers of Danu would never stoop so low as to run someone off the road. I just needed you to believe they would so that you wouldn't trust them. Of course, they didn't do themselves any favours when they got themselves caught up in the abduction attempt I'd planned on Saturday. So, after that, it was really just a case of feeding the fear."

He rubbed the back of his neck with a mock grimace. "I'd have preferred to avoid the crash myself – I really loved that car. But what better way to get you to trust me? And your own guilt did the rest for me."

I shook my head, not wanting to believe it. "Why?"

"I needed you to do the ritual. Do you know how long we've been waiting for this? How long *I've* been waiting? I thought the visions might have been enough to get you on board, but you were too stubborn to make it easy. I probably shouldn't have been surprised, given your bloodline."

"My bloodline ..." The Tuatha. Siobhán had told me; I just hadn't wanted to listen.

Tears burned the back of my eyes and I balled my hands into fists. He'd played me like a fool, and I'd let him. How could I have been so damn stupid?

Brian's words about the magic came back to me then, and a terrifying cold settled over me. "What did the ritual really do?"

"You mean what did you do?" He grinned and walked onto the scorched earth, coming to a stop before me. He leaned in, his breath tickling my cheek as he whispered conspiratorially in my ear, "You released the magic."

He gave me a kiss on the cheek and stepped back, leaving me to stare in numb shock. "You did good, Aisling. Don't be too hard on yourself. I mean, who wouldn't have fallen for these charms?"

With a wink, he turned and strolled casually back towards the wall that separated the field from the church grounds. He spared Siobhán and Brian another unconcerned glance as he passed them and paused to look back at me.

"For what it's worth, they're not dead. They'll wake up at some point."

I could've sworn he muttered, "More's the pity," under his breath as he turned and walked away, leaving me standing alone in the middle of the stone circle, wondering what the hell I'd just done.

Like the coward I was, I ran. I took the book and the box, I got into my car, and I drove away from that damned field so fast I almost careened into another ditch.

I'd checked to make sure Siobhán and Brian really were alive before leaving. It had taken me a lot longer than I was willing to admit to make my feet move towards their prone bodies, but I wasn't willing to take Bres at his word – never again.

An anonymous phone call for an ambulance did little to assuage my guilty conscience, but when both had begun to stir, I couldn't face seeing the truth of my stupidity reflected back at me in their expressions. So, I ran.

Maybe if I could put enough distance between myself and that place, I could believe this whole thing had been a bad dream? That I hadn't really been such a gullible fool...

But the whole way home, Bres's words repeated over and over in my head: *You released the magic.*

It was just another part of his games. Magic didn't exist. He clearly got some kind of sick, twisted enjoyment out of messing with people's heads, and I'd just been unlucky enough to be his most recent target.

Of course, that didn't explain the illusion spell or the stone circle. It didn't explain my dreams. And it didn't explain the dreadful certainty that gnawed away at my chest now.

The drive home was a blur. My hands were still shaking uncontrollably by the time I reached the door to Teagan's apartment, and I fumbled as I tried to get the key into the lock for the third time. The key slipped from my fingers and clattered to the floor. I swore, tears burning the back of my eyes.

The door swung open to reveal Teagan brandishing her largest kitchen knife and looking ready to gut someone. Her eyes widened in alarm as she took in my dishevelled state. Abandoning the knife on the small hall table, she grabbed my elbow and helped me inside.

"Jesus, Aisling. Where the hell have you been? You look like shit."

A small laugh escaped my throat, and even to my own ears it sounded slightly hysterical. I let her lead me into the living area and deposit me on the sofa, not sure my legs would have carried me there without the support.

Clearly noticing that I was shivering, Teagan

hurried over and filled the kettle. I had no idea how much time passed, but the next thing I knew I was being handed a steaming mug of tea that contained so much sugar the sweet aroma tickled my nose.

"Drink," she ordered, sitting down beside me.

I raised the mug to my lips, but though I swallowed a mouthful, I couldn't have said whether the contents were scalding hot or ice cold.

A weighty silence stretched out between us. Teagan was clearly giving me a chance to compose myself, but the determined set to her jaw overshadowed the concern in her blue eyes, and I knew she wouldn't be patient for long.

What could I tell her that she would possibly believe? Hell, I didn't even believe it myself.

The tears that had threatened, finally spilled over. I placed my mug on the coffee table and buried my face in my hands.

Teagan pulled me into her arms. "Dammit, Aisling. Talk to me. Please." Her voice cracked on the last word, and my heart broke for the pain I was causing her.

"Is it Bres, that guy you've been seeing? Did something happen? Did he do something?"

I shook my head and wiped my snotty nose with the back of my hand. I was exhausted. Empty. And I had no idea where to start.

"It's not like that. I promise." I took a shuddering breath and let the numbness envelope me. "Do you mind if I just go to bed? I swear I'll tell you everything." Or at least I'd try. "I just need to rest."

Teagan's mouth settled in an unhappy line, but she wrapped an arm around my waist and led me into my bedroom. She helped me strip off my clothes and tucked the blankets in tight around me, brushing the hair away from my face.

"We're going to talk about this as soon as you wake up," she warned. Then her voice softened. "Call me if you need anything."

My eyes slid closed before she'd shut the bedroom door.

The field I found myself in this time was different from the one I'd left behind only a couple of hours previous. There were no standing stones, and the ground was covered in a lush grass instead of the charred earth that had been stained by my blood.

A soft breeze rustled through the nearby trees, and I was acutely aware of the sounds of wildlife nearby: the skittering of the field mouse, the soft chirp of the baby birds waiting for their mother to return with food, the squirrel as it gnawed on its hard-earned bounty. Everything felt so alive and vibrant.

Footsteps crunched on the grass, and I swung around, my heart racing in sudden panic.

The man who approached was unfamiliar to me, and stupidly, that fact allowed me to relax somewhat. His light brown hair was brushed carelessly back behind one ear and reached almost to the jaw that was coated in days-old stubble. A black shirt hung open over a white t-shirt, and with his faded ripped jeans, he looked as out of place in the peaceful field as I felt.

He came to a stop beside me and stared into the distance with his hands in his back pockets.

"You've really fucked it now."

I jerked back as if he'd slapped me. "Excuse me?"

"The magic," he said. "Can't you feel it? It'll take time, but make no mistake, it's coming. I hope you're ready."

<<<<<>>>>>

You've seen it through Aisling's eyes. Now, relive their first meeting through Bres's...

Sign up to my Newsletter and get your exclusive bonus scene now!

https://books.lmhatchell.com/jl52sql8go

READ ON FOR A PREVIEW OF...

THE GUARDIAN'S LEGACY

Celtic Curses, Book 2

CHAPTER 1

Four weeks. That was how long had passed since I'd fucked up and released magic back into Ireland. So I'd been told, at least. I'd yet to see a single rainstorm of toads, blood moon, or hell, even a rabbit pop out of a hat to prove that was true.

As I closed the deposition I'd been typing up for my boss, I couldn't help but wonder what it would be like if that magic was real. I wouldn't be stuck here looking at the same boring legal stuff day in day out, that was for sure.

"Aisling, good, you're still here. I need you to do something for me."

I froze, a fraction of a second away from shutting down my computer when my boss's nasally voice smashed any hopes I had of escaping at a reasonable time. Overcome with the urge to bang my head against the desk, I clamped my lips shut against the groan that threatened to escape and turned to face Clifford Mercer.

Smith & Mercer is a highly prestigious law firm. You're lucky to work for them. This is just one more step towards the promotion you've been promised. I repeated the mantra silently to myself and waited with a carefully schooled expression to see what fun task was in store for me on this fine Thursday evening.

Tall and reedy with pinched features, my boss bore a remarkable resemblance to a weasel. The comparison was only heightened further by his personality, but as he was one of the founding partners of the firm, I made a point of keeping that opinion to myself.

Clifford thrust a thin manila envelope at me. "I need you to entertain a client. Mr. Athanosios is coming in to collect this, and I need you to take him out to dinner. This deal is very important, so see to it that he's looked after."

"This evening?" I croaked, failing to keep the incredulity from my voice despite my best efforts.

I was used to my boss taking liberties, but this was really taking the piss. It was five o'clock for god's sake, and he was telling me now? For all he knew, I already had plans for the evening. I didn't, but that wasn't the point.

"When else?" he asked, clearly oblivious to my irritation.

Not waiting for me to respond, he snatched his briefcase up from the floor and strode for the door. "Make sure to turn off the lights when you're leaving," he called over his shoulder. "The energy bills are criminal these days."

With that parting instruction, he disappeared, no doubt on his way to the six-figure diesel-guzzling car he kept in a private parking space below the office block – a space that likely cost more than my annual salary to rent given our offices were in the heart of Dublin city centre.

I gaped at the now empty doorway, wondering what the hell had just happened. How had I gotten stuck with entertainment duty? Surely if the client was so important, Clifford should bloody well be the one to take him to dinner.

Not for the first time, I thought about walking out and never looking back.

I'd strongly considered it after the whole magic fiasco last month – resigning, starting fresh somewhere new.

Not that Smith & Mercer had any part to play in my screw-up, really. But the firm represented the Order of the Fomori, a modern-day society that stemmed from the ancient race of the Fomorians. And the Order most definitely had played a part. A very big one.

Descending from the Tuatha Dé Danann, my family line had apparently been assigned the role of Guardian to Ireland's magic. The Tuatha sacrificed most of their own race to stop their sworn enemies, the Fomorians, from claiming it, and I, being the current Guardian, was meant to ensure that sacrifice hadn't been made in vain.

Of course, nobody bothered to bloody tell me any of that. So, when a trip to an old graveyard resulted in a seizure and some not so fun nightly visions, the Order took advantage of my ignorance by sending in Bres, their most charming representative.

He convinced me that the Tuatha Dé Danann were evil, that they were trying to use me to regain access to our world so they could enslave us all. He failed to mention that he was a lying sack of shit, and the ritual he wanted me to conduct to stop them would actually release the magic I was meant to safeguard.

Since I'd discovered the truth – too late – on the summer solstice, anything that made me think of Bres or the Order only served as an uncomfortable reminder of my naivety. Smith & Mercer fell into that category, and the sickening twist of shame that followed me into the office every day had almost been enough to make me quit.

Unfortunately, pride was one thing; money was another. And I didn't have the luxury of ignoring the latter.

So, I sat staring at the glowing screen of my computer as it mocked me for once again being a doormat. Well, screw this. I might have to give up my evening to babysit one of our pompous, rich clients, but I wasn't going to make myself useful while I waited.

For the second time, I moved to switch my computer off. A polite clearing of the throat stopped me in my tracks, and I yelped in surprise.

"Apologies. I didn't mean to startle you."

I jerked my head up to find a man with tanned skin and eyes as dark as his finely tailored charcoal suit watching me from the doorway. He was cleanly shaven and not a strand of his black hair dared to move out of place. A hint of amusement tugged at the corner of his lips, reducing the weight of his imposing presence only marginally.

Flustered, I pushed back from my desk and stood, offering my hand in greeting. "Mr. Athanosios?"

The man inclined his head and strode into the office to shake it. His grip was neither limp – the worst kind of handshake – nor did he try to demonstrate the size of his dick by crushing the bones of my hand. He went up marginally in my esteem for this, but as I was still irritated at Clifford's decision to effectively pimp me out, I refused to let myself be impressed.

During my time with the firm, I'd met many of our V.I.P. clients. The man before me didn't look familiar, and I was vaguely curious as to what could be important enough for him to traipse across the city to collect an envelope himself. A courier could've easily been arranged – and I wouldn't have been expected to wine and dine *them*.

I pushed the thought away before it could show on my face and held the envelope out to him. There was nothing on the outside to give away the contents, just a single word stamped in bold text: *Confidential*.

"I believe this is for you."

He didn't even glance at it as he took it, instead

seeming to assess me. "Please, call me Dothur. I do apologise for inconveniencing your evening..."

"Aisling," I supplied.

"Aisling." He rolled my name on his tongue, his smooth accent making it sound impossibly exotic. "Well, Aisling, I've been informed that you are my chaperone for the evening?"

I pasted what I hoped was a professional smile on my face and reached for my bag. It really wasn't the client's fault that my boss was a dick; there was no point taking my irritation out on him.

Dothur watched me with a contemplative gaze as I – finally – switched off my computer.

"While I would be honoured to have the company of a lovely lady such as yourself for dinner, I can't help but feel it's unfair of your firm to place this require-ment on you," he observed.

"We're always happy to accommodate our clients." *Ugh, I think I just puked in my mouth a little.*

A quirked eyebrow and flash of amusement in his dark eyes told me he didn't buy my bullshit any more than I did. "Be that as it may, if you have other plans for the evening, I would be happy to free you from this obligation. Your boss need not know."

I eyed him suspiciously. Nothing about his expres-sion suggested he was being anything other than genuine in his offer, but it seemed a little too good to be true. Was he really giving me the chance to gracefully bow out and avoid an awkward evening of small talk?

He waited patiently while I waged my internal

debate, and I grudgingly allocated him some extra brownie points for not being pushy.

Teagan, my best friend, lectured on ancient civilisations to her adult night class on Thursdays. Since she'd kindly donated her spare room until I got back on my feet after a breakup, I'd be going home to an empty apartment to heat up leftover curry for one. Not exactly a wild night.

Or … I could go to dinner with him.

Admittedly, he was quite handsome, and while the dinner would be purely business, it never hurt to have a nice view while I was doing my duty as the obedient paralegal. Besides, Clifford would no doubt grill me tomorrow, and even if Dothur kept quiet about me bailing, my boss would sniff out the lie in a matter of minutes.

Before I could rethink, I found myself saying, "We can't have a valued client eating alone, now can we?"

More than one pair of female eyes followed Dothur with interest as a waiter led us to a table at the back of the small restaurant. The looks I got as his companion of choice were less friendly.

The Millstone had a charming rustic décor, and the soft glow of candlelight gave the place a more romantic atmosphere than I'd envisaged when agreeing to dinner. Still, I'd heard good things about the restaurant, and I couldn't deny that my companion for the evening looked pretty tasty, too.

I gave the waiter a polite smile as he pulled out my chair and set menus in front of us.

"We'll have the smoked salmon to start. The fillet steak, medium rare," Dothur said, as soon as the man had finished reeling off the specials. "And a bottle of Châteauneuf-du-Pape."

He handed the menus back before I'd even had a chance to open mine, and the waiter scurried off, carefully avoiding my surprised gaze.

I raised an eyebrow. "Bit presumptuous. How do you know I like any of those things?"

Dothur gave me a devilish wink, unperturbed. "Because you're a lady of good taste."

I crossed my arms and fought to keep my expression unimpressed despite the smile that set my lips twitching. "I could have a fatal allergy to fish for all you know."

"Do you?"

"No, but I could."

"I'd be happy to administer CPR if you need it."

I froze, my breath stalling at the comment.

It hadn't been so long ago that Bres had playfully offered me his CPR services. He'd been handsome and charming too, and I'd let it cloud my judgement. Maybe this had been a mistake. Maybe I shouldn't be here.

Dothur frowned, clearly noticing my reaction. "If

you're concerned about an allergic reaction, we can order something else."

What? Oh.

I snapped out of my morose thoughts, annoyed with myself. What was I doing? Dothur wasn't Bres. He'd been nothing but polite and charming, and here I was freaking out about a perfectly innocent comment. *Dammit, Aisling, at least try to leave your crazy at the door for one night.*

With what I hoped was a reassuring smile, I shook my head and laughed. "Sorry. No, what you ordered is fine." I smoothed the pristine white tablecloth out in front of me, squirming self-consciously under the weight of his dark gaze.

Thankfully, the waiter chose that moment to return with our bottle of wine, shifting the attention from me. He presented the bottle to Dothur for approval. "Would Sir care to sample it first?"

Dothur waved away the offer, and the waiter proceeded to pour the wine. I watched the ruby liquid slosh into my glass and silently hoped that I could make it through the dinner without spilling it on the beautiful tablecloth.

"So, where are you from, Dothur?" I asked once the waiter was finished and had scurried away again. "That's definitely not an Irish accent."

His lips quirked up at my genius observation. "Indeed. I'm from Greece. My brothers and I are here for a few weeks on business."

"Oh, really? Can I ask what kind of business?"

"It's a family business. We deal in natural energies."

I took a sip of my wine and winced a little at the vinegary taste. Would he be insulted if I ordered a different drink?

"Interesting," I said, pushing the glass away – I'd stick to water. "Did your brothers come to Ireland with you?"

"Yes. Ireland has a special place in my family's history, so when the opportunity arose to return, we couldn't turn it down."

"Oh, you've been here before?"

"A long time ago. Tell me about yourself, Aisling."

His dark eyes met mine, and I felt my cheeks heat as he focused the full weight of his attention on me.

"Not much to tell." I shrugged a little self-consciously. "I'm a Dublin girl, born and bred. I've worked for Smith & Mercer for three years, though I always secretly wanted to join the circus. But shh, don't tell anyone," I told him with a conspiratorial whisper.

He laughed at that, a rich, sensuous sound that sent a shiver of delight through me.

I had to give it to the man, he was the personification of sexy. Tall, dark, and handsome, wrapped up in a well-dressed package, and finished off with a yummy accent. I could almost forgive Clifford for dumping this dinner on me last minute. Almost.

The waiter returned then with our starters in hand, and for a few minutes we ate in companionable silence. I caught Dothur watching my reaction more than once, but I stoically refused to let him see just how much I was enjoying his choice. Admittedly, though, it was some of the nicest smoked salmon I'd ever tasted.

"What about your family? Are they from here also?" Dothur asked before taking a sip of his wine – I couldn't help but notice that he didn't wince at the taste.

"Yep, one hundred per cent Irish." I dabbed my mouth with my cloth napkin and pushed away my empty plate. "My mam was born in Wicklow and has never left since. She and my dad separated when I was a baby, so I don't remember much about him, but I believe he was from Dublin."

"No siblings?"

"Nope, only child. Teagan, my best friend, is the closest thing I have to a sister, though I always wanted a brother when I was younger. Are you and your brothers close?"

He tilted his head, considering the question. "Sometimes it feels like we've spent many lifetimes together. It makes for both an unbreakable bond and a regular desire to, how do you say, throttle each other."

I snorted out a very unladylike laugh at his choice of phrase, the sensual accent making it sound completely out of place. "Sounds like an interesting dynamic."

He gave a wry smile. "Family. Can't live with them, can't live without them."

CHAPTER 2

A gentle breeze ruffled my hair, and I raised my face to the warm sun that shone overhead. Somewhere in the distance, birds chirped and the trees whispered their secrets to each other. The meadow I sat in was surrounded by rolling hills as far as the eye could see, and the grass beneath me was so soft that if I closed my eyes I could almost imagine I was floating on a cloud.

None of this should have been possible, of course. The heat of the sun shouldn't have rejuvenated me the way it did. I shouldn't have been able to run my fingers through the rich, green grass, and nature's fragrant aroma shouldn't have drifted to me on the breeze. Because this was all a dream.

Almost every night for the four weeks that had passed since the solstice, I'd found myself here in this place. It had become almost as real to me as the waking world, though logically I knew that was crazy. Still, the calm of my surroundings lulled me into a state of relaxation, my mind drifting to memories of my dinner with Dothur.

As it turned out, the evening had been very enjoyable. Dothur had managed to find quite an appealing balance between being intriguing and cultured, while also showing genuine interest in my more mundane life. He'd apparently enjoyed our time together too, as we parted with him asking for my phone number. I knew it wasn't wise to get involved with a client of the firm, but he was only in town for a few weeks. What was the harm in a bit of fun?

"You're not concentrating."

I cracked an eye open to find Killian slouched against a nearby tree with his arms crossed, an expression of bemused exasperation on his face.

My dream mentor ran a hand through his light brown jaw-length hair, clearly trying to rein in his frustration at his wayward student. As always, he wore faded jeans and a black shirt with the sleeves rolled up. I'd asked him once where he got the clothes from, since fashion had changed drastically from the time the Tuatha Dé Danann – and therefore, he – had last roamed our world. He'd cryptically said something about appearing to me in whatever form made it most likely for my mind to accept his presence. The idea had hurt my head and raised even more questions than it answered, which was not helpful in the slightest.

"It's hard to concentrate with you staring at me," I pointed out, though in truth I'd been so lost in my thoughts that I hadn't even realised he'd arrived. "What's the lesson for today, boss?"

"Meditation."

I groaned. We'd been at this meditation crap for weeks now, and I still sucked at it. Seriously, how was it possible to empty your mind and think of nothing? The very fact of telling yourself to stop thinking produced a thought in itself; it made no sense to me.

Still, Killian was the magic expert, so as always, I humoured him and closed my eyes.

"Clear your mind," he instructed, and instantly thoughts multiplied in my head like horny bunny rabbits having an orgy. "Listen to the world around you. Feel it. Let its energy wash over you, fill you."

I focused on the low, soothing cadence of his voice, and slowly the thoughts faded away.

"You are the Guardian," he continued. "Your very being connects you to the magic. You just have to open yourself to it."

Open myself. Sure, I can do that. I'm an open door.

As I had many, many times before, I waited. What I was waiting for, I didn't really know. A bolt of lightning? A glowing light bulb to appear over my head? A sudden shifting of my world view that would make me wonder how I'd been so blind up to this point?

But just like every other time, nothing happened.

With a huff of frustration, I flung myself back on the grass and opened my eyes. "Do we have to keep doing this? It's been a month. Surely we'd know by now if the magic was back?"

There was a long silence before I sensed Killian move to my side. He sat down next to me, draped his arms over his bent knees, and stared out into the distance.

"The magic is back. I wouldn't be here with you now if it wasn't. But things are very different in your world now."

My world. I didn't miss the phrasing, or the careful way he kept his tone neutral as he said it.

It had once been his world too. A very long time ago.

Just as my role of Guardian had been built into the sacrificial ritual conducted by the Tuatha Dé Danann, so too had Killian's. He was a fail-safe of sorts. It was the Guardian's job to protect the gateway to the magic. Killian's was to deal with the fallout should the Guardian fail.

He'd told me this when he'd first come to me in my dreams. Actually, his exact words to me had been, "You've really fucked it now," but then he'd at least proceeded to fill in some of the many gaps in my knowledge.

What he hadn't told me was why he'd volunteered for the role. Considering it had resulted in him being held in stasis for millennia before finally being awoken thanks to my naivety, I couldn't help but be curious about his motives.

"What do you mean things are different?" I asked.

"The technological advancements that have been made are nothing short of magical in themselves, but they are man-made. The destruction of nature for the sake of progression has changed things, and it will impact the speed and form in which magic returns. The only question is how."

"If all these advancements are such a big block, how can you be sure it will return at all? Maybe the ritual did work, but the magic just isn't strong enough to overcome the changes?"

The corner of his lip twitched with amusement he was clearly trying to contain, and I scowled at him.

"The magic is tied to the land. The land will always be stronger, no matter how much the ignorance of man damages it."

I thought of the natural disasters that were occurring more and more frequently around the world, and I found I couldn't quite disagree with his point. Even in Ireland the signs of global warming were becoming visible on a daily basis, and I'd often wondered how much of it was nature fighting back against our so-called progress.

When I didn't argue, Killian gave me a considering look. He extended his hand and slowly rotated it from side to side. Sparks of green light crackled and skittered along his skin. It appeared almost like electricity, but he didn't flinch at its touch, so I had to assume it wasn't hurting him.

"The magic is in its purest form here," he said, staring at the light. "Frozen at the point in time just before the Tuatha sacrificed themselves to protect it." He snapped his hand closed and the sparks winked out. "But if you don't believe, it might as well not exist at all."

Silence settled between us as I considered his words. He made it sound so simple; just believe, and *poof!* Magic. That was all well and good, but what if I never got the hang of it? Sure, I was the Guardian, but I'd already proved I sucked at that, so who was to say I wouldn't suck at this magic craic too?

I pushed myself back up to sitting and huffed out a breath. "Is it really so bad if I can't use it? I mean, let's say the magic has returned and I never manage to access it. Does it really make a difference?"

"When magic was last part of your world, the Fomorians stopped at nothing to control it. Do you think the Order of the Fomori will be any different? Times may have moved on, and their methods may have changed, but I can guarantee you they haven't. They've used you once to get what they wanted. They'll do it again."

My throat burned at the reminder of how I'd allowed myself to be manipulated.

When Bres first approached me, I'd been convinced he was a conman. No matter how sexy and charming as he was, talk of ancient races and magical visions would be enough to send any woman running a mile. But then the visions – or dreams, as I'd thought them to be – started taking their toll on me. I'd have done anything to make them stop.

Since the Watchers of Danu, what remained now of the Tuatha lineage, hadn't bothered to clue me in on my heritage, I'd thought I was going nuts. And when Bres offered me not just proof of his tale, but also a solution to save my sanity, I'd left all reason at the door and followed him blindly to the conclusion he'd been steering me towards all along.

The visions had stopped as soon as I completed the ritual; that much he'd been honest about, at least. Instead, they'd been replaced by nightly magic lessons with Killian in this dreamscape. It was safe to say I was a pretty crap student, though maybe if I got a cool wand or something I'd feel motivated to try harder.

As it was, I brushed off his comment with barely concealed vehemence. "I won't be stupid enough to fall for their lies again."

Shadows darkened his brown eyes and he turned his gaze away from me. "There are many ways to mislead with the truth, too."

I searched his expression but found it as unreadable as ever. I sighed.

"They haven't come near me since the solstice. They got what they wanted. Surely I'm of less use to them if I stay magically impotent."

In fact, nobody had come near me since the solstice – not the Order, and not the Watchers of Danu. The former was a welcome relief, the latter downright pissed me off.

The Watchers had known all along that I was the Guardian and had left me to flounder in my ignorance until it was too late. They'd claimed not to want to burden me with the responsibility unless it was absolutely necessary. What was their excuse now?

Killian pushed himself up from the ground and offered me his hand with a crooked smile that didn't quite chase the shadows from his eyes. "Humour me."

Huffing to ensure my martyrdom was clear, I accepted it and stood.

"Close your eyes," he ordered, and I did.

The heat of his touch caused my skin to tingle, and the rhythmic flow of his words lulled me back into that relaxed state. I allowed my mind to drift, considering what it might actually be like to have magic.

Killian had explained that magic came from the life force of all living things. In humans, it took different forms depending on a person's natural affinity, but in theory, we all held that energy inside us. Accessing it was a whole different ball game, however.

The thought drifted away as Killian guided me through the now-familiar meditation. My breathing relaxed and my body became heavy as my weight sank down into the earth, grounding me. Bit by bit, the tension left my body.

The gentle tug beneath my belly button was so subtle that at first I thought my imagination was playing tricks on me. It was an odd sensation, almost like a rope that connected me to something unseen.

My eyes flew open. "I think –"

As quickly as it had come, the feeling disappeared. I pressed my hand to my abdomen, looking down in wonder. Had I imagined it?

I opened my mouth to voice the question aloud, but before I could speak, an alarm clock blared. The meadow dissolved around me, taking with it whatever tenuous thread I may or may not have discovered to the magic.

<<<<<>>>>>

GET IT NOW!

ABOUT THE AUTHOR

Thank you for joining me on this adventure through Ireland's hidden (for now) supernatural world. This is entirely a work of fiction, so while I have taken inspiration from well known Celtic myths, I hope you'll allow me some poetic license with these as I build this new and exciting world.

If you enjoyed this book, I would be very grateful if you could leave a brief review (it can be as short as you like) on the site where you purchased your copy.

As an author, reviews are the most powerful tools in my arsenal when it comes to getting attention for my books. Honest feedback goes a long way in increasing visibility and helping me to reach other readers like you, so thank you in advance!

*To get exclusive bonus material and be the first to hear about new releases, promotions, and giveaways **Sign up for my Newsletter** at https://lmhatchell.com*

ALSO BY L.M. HATCHELL

To see the latest on all my books and upcoming publications, visit

https://lmhatchell.com/books

9 781916 365162